The Ghost of Meriwether Manor

By

Emily Beaver

The Ghost of Meriwether Manor
Copyright © 2010 by Emily Beaver
Meriwether Mystery Series Book 3

Original Illustrations by Joy Noguess

All rights reserved. No part of the work may be reproduced or transmitted in any form or by any means, electronic or mechanical, including photocopying, recording, scanning or otherwise, or by any storage or retrieval system, except as may be expressly permitted by the 1976 Copyright Act, or in writing from the author.

Requests for permission should be made in writing to:

Smooth Sailing Press
Attn: Publisher
PO Box 1439 / Tomball, Texas 77377
9306 Max Conrad Drive / Suite C / Spring, Texas 77379

Printed in China

ISBN 978-1-933660-43-1

SMOOTH SAILING PRESS
(281) 251-0830 / www.smoothsailingpress.com

*...For Emma, Jay Riley, and Nathan
. . . my inspiration.*

Chapter One

Brrring . . . brrring . . . the sturdy black telephone rang shrilled from its place beside her bed. She had been asleep, but was now instantly awake, "Hello?"

"It's time, Miss Morrow," said a shaky voice on the other end of the line.

She threw off her covers and dressed as quickly as she could, fingers fumbling with coat buttons in the cold of the room. She twisted her long blonde hair away from both sides of her face and pinned it back so that the waves cascaded down her back. Even in her haste, she frowned at herself in the mirror, and with trembling hands applied a layer of red lipstick to her thin mouth.

The car groaned and sputtered, but eventually the engine turned over. Her heart was in her throat. *Just a bit longer, now,* she told herself.

Screeching to a halt on the gravely drive, she flung open the great wooden doors without waiting to be let in and ran up the stairs. Smoothing her hair, she approached the man sitting on a high-backed bench in the hall. His head was bent and his fingers laced together on his knees as if he were praying. He looked up and smiled wearily, "Dr. Willowsby is with her. Thank you for coming, Lydia."

She wanted to reach out and comfort him, but she didn't dare. Instead she said, "We may have a long night of it. Can I make you some tea?"

He nodded absently. She wasn't sure he had even heard her . . . but it was something to do.

Meriwether Manor

She hurried with the tea things and loaded a silver tray with a steaming pot, cups, saucers, and a plate of hot buttered toast. She unbuttoned her coat but left it on. The kitchen was cold, and her dress was thin. Her fingers felt like icicles, and she was worried. The baby wasn't supposed to come for another few weeks.

When she got back upstairs, Lionel was pacing, arms behind his back, up and down the hall. He was fully dressed, as if he'd never gone to bed -- which he probably hadn't -- she knew he often stayed up late into the night, holed away in his study. He sank heavily back onto the bench, his sandy hair mussed and pushed carelessly away from his ruddy, handsome face; strong shoulders hunched, hands clasped against his knees.

"I don't know what I'll do if I lose her, Lydia," he said in a low voice.

Her stomach did a funny sort of leap. "Everything will be fine, Lionel. You'll see."

He went on as if she hadn't said anything, "She's become . . . so dear . . . these last few months . . . she's different somehow . . . have you noticed? . . . and . . . I . . . I . . . I'm terrified of losing her." He crumpled, head in his hands. His shoulders shook with raw emotion.

Feet moving like lead, she approached him, patting him on the back awkwardly. "Don't worry. Lillian will be fine. The baby will be fine," she said in rote, her heart a stone in her chest.

Deep into the night they waited. At last, they heard a blessed, bleating cry and knew that the baby, at least, was well. Minutes later, young Dr. Willowsby, mopping his brow with a handkerchief, shirt sleeves rolled up past his elbows, came out of the room and shook Lionel's hand,

"Congratulations, man. You have a beautiful baby girl."

Lionel beamed, "And Lillian? How's Lillian?"

"Fine, fine," Dr. Willowsby assured him. "Go on in. See your new family," he said as Lionel's head bobbed up and down in gratitude. "Hello, Lydia."

"Samuel," she said primly as his eyes regarded her with interest.

"Incredible," he said, shaking his head.

"What is?"

"Absolutely identical. One of you should cut your hair or something, else I don't know how anyone could ever tell the two of you apart."

"I'll keep that in mind," she answered icily. "Now, if you'll excuse me, I must see my sister and my new niece." She sailed round him and into the bedroom. Lionel sat on the bed beside her sister, the baby cradled in her arms, a pretty little vignette illuminated in the soft glow of the bed lamp. The sisters' eyes met, and a slow, fat tear fell down the mother's white cheek.

Chapter Two

Gazing up at her father under a fringe of dark lashes, Meriwether slit open the envelope with trembling fingers. She'd often wondered why her parents had named her Meriwether. Now, she thought she knew. Dr. Knight's scowl deepened as she smoothed out the thick, robin's egg blue parchment. She turned away from him slightly, letting her hair swing down in front of her face for privacy.

Dear Meriwether,

Your grandfather has taken ill and insists upon meeting you. I realize you have school, but I feel confident that something suitable can be arranged. If Mrs. Knight is amenable, I shall begin interviewing eligible tutors post haste. We will expect you on the morning train, to Hawkshead, 1 October.

Sincerely,

Lillian Meriwether

For some minutes, Meriwether studied the letter in confusion, and not a small bit of pique. A summons is what it was. Her presence was required, and so she must come. Never mind that she was on the volleyball team. Never mind that Holly would probably murder her for skipping out on her yet again. Never mind that she'd not heard from her mother's family even once in her entire life!

No, the Meriwether's had never made the slightest attempt to communicate with their granddaughter. They had, in fact, ignored her existence completely, having cut all relations with their only daughter -- Meriwether's mother -- when she married *the American*. Even when Felicia was diagnosed with cancer, even when she refused treatment until her child was born . . . still they maintained their frozen disapproval, their deafening silence, their absolute absence.

And now she was just supposed to pack up and fly

off to her ailing grandfather? Where had he been as her mother lay on her own death bed? Cold, hard anger ran like ice in Meriwether's veins. Without looking at her father, she held the letter out to him. He read it as Meriwether fought to gain control of her emotions.

It was a short note, but Dr. Knight held it for a long time. No longer scowling, his face was impassive as stone. Meriwether thought she knew what he must be thinking, so she was surprised when he finally spoke, "I think you should go."

"You think I should what?!!!" coughed Meriwether.

"You should go to your grandfather," Dr. Knight repeated evenly. Meriwether thought he sounded as if he'd been hypnotized.

This was too much! Meriwether had been sure her father would be on her side. How could he possibly approve of sending her off to the horrible people who had treated them all so cruelly?

"This is your chance, Meriwether. Your chance to meet your mother's family . . . to fix what was broken. If Colonel Meriwether wants to meet you, then you should go. You may never get another shot." Meriwether knew her father was remembering his own missed chance to make amends before his father's death. After years of stubborn silence, he had only very recently patched things up with Grandmother.

"But what about . . . about," Meriwether stammered, trying to think of an appropriate epithet for Mrs. Meriwether.

Her father read her mind. "Now if you can warm up to the *Snow Queen*, you'll deserve a medal. I wouldn't go expecting much from her. Just do as she says, and stay out of her way. You should be fine." To the deflated look on Meriwether's face he added, "Don't worry, you won't be alone."

Meriwether brightened immediately, "You'll go with me?"

"Oh, no," Dr. Knight was quick to make that clear, "but I have something in mind that should cheer you up."

Certain her Grandmother would put a stop to this nonsense; Meriwether was shocked to learn that she too agreed with Dr. Knight.

"But . . . but," stammered Meriwether.

"No buts," said her Grandmother firmly, one eyebrow arched into a familiar look that Meriwether knew brooked no argument.

October 1st, was just around the corner, and the temperatures were still soaring in Texas. It had been a long, dry summer. The June rains had forgotten to come, so everything was suffering from the endless sun and heat. Meriwether much preferred the cools of spring and autumn, so as she packed, with her best friend Holly sitting Indian style on the bed and staring up at her mournfully, Meriwether contented herself with mental images of herself in sweaters and jackets, exploring the centuries old manor house her father had described.

He refused to share with Meriwether what he had up his sleeve . . . the thing that should cheer her up. He said he wanted to make sure it was going to work out before he said anymore.

"Promise you'll write?" Holly tucked a thin strand of blonde bob behind one ear and flapped her folded up legs like a big brown butterfly.

"Of course I'll write!" snapped Meriwether, a little more sharply than she'd intended. Holly's deep blue eyes widened into O's. "Promise *you'll* write?"

Holly dropped her gaze, "Oh, yeah . . . sorry about that."

Just a few months ago, Meriwether had made her first trip (in memory) across the pond that separated her from the land of her birth. Small town West Texas, with Grandmother as her guardian, was the home she had always known, but her life had begun in the ancient city of Oxford, England.

When Grandmother had suffered a serious heart attack at the beginning of summer vacation, she'd sent Meriwether to her father, archaeologist and restorations expert, Dr. Peter Knight. An old secret had kept Dr. Knight away from his family for many years, but Meriwether had helped to set things straight. In fact, her father had returned with Meriwether to Sterling City, and they were just off the tail end of settling yet another mystery.

All in all, Meriwether had been very busy.

Holly had been no slouch.

Over the summer she had managed to fall in a major crush (the reason she hardly ever wrote Meriwether back), get her heart broken, and help Meriwether solve the mystery of the cave. She had been excited for Meriwether to go to England in the first place and get to know her father, even though she had hoped Meriwether might get to stay with them in Texas for the summer, but now she felt as if she were being abandoned. Oh, she knew it wasn't Meriwether's fault . . . even knew Meriwether would rather not go. All the same, here she was, packing up to leave on another adventure, leaving Holly home to hold down the fort. She would give anything she owned to go with her.

"Sorry," Meriwether sat down beside Holly on the bed and put her head on her friend's shoulder.

Holly bent her head and rested it on Meriwether's shining auburn waves. "I know," she whispered, wiping at a lone tear that had managed its way down her cheek.

Chapter Three

Early on the morning of September 28th, Mr. Hart, Holly's father and editor of the local paper, drove Dr. Knight, Meriwether, and Holly -- who had begged off a day of school -- to the Midland airport. From there, they would fly to Dallas, connect to New York's JFK, then on to London. It was a lot of starting and stopping, but they had decided it would be easier to make the hour's drive to Midland than the four plus one to Dallas.

Mr. Hart had offered his services as chauffer, and Grandmother, who doubted the ability of the Hart's vehicle to make the journey without incident, volunteered her Cadillac as transport. Meriwether and her father had gladly accepted the arrangement.

Mr. Hart and Dr. Knight sat up front talking easily, and Meriwether and Holly sat in the back silently holding hands. Meriwether was armed with lesson plans for the next few weeks and a special waver from Mr. Coulter, the school superintendent, for excessive absences. Meriwether's . . . *grandmother?* . . . no that was too weird . . . *Mrs. Meriwether* had been very vague as to how long Meriwether was expected to stay. Meriwether hoped she would be back before the lesson plans ran out.

As apprehensive as Meriwether was to visit her

estranged relatives, she was very excited to get to see Daniel and Mrs. Doone again. Mrs. Doone was her father's little Welsh housekeeper in Oxford, and Daniel was her grandson. Meriwether and Daniel had become fast friends earlier that summer, and Meriwether had missed him terribly. She knew he knew she was coming because Dr. Knight had been in close contact with Mrs. Doone about arrival times and schedules -- that sort of thing.

Maybe Daniel could visit her in Hawkshead. Meriwether decided to ask him about it when they got to her father's home in Oxford.

Mr. Hart dropped Meriwether and her father off curbside at the airport. Mr. Hart and Dr. Knight shook hands, "Thanks Martin . . . appreciate the lift!"

"No problem," smiled Mr. Hart. "Meriwether, you take care of yourself, you hear?"

Meriwether nodded as Mr. Hart clapped her shoulder in a sideways hug, "I will."

Holly and Meriwether stared at one another solemnly. "See you soon?" murmured Meriwether.

Holly bit her bottom lip and smiled a watery smile, "Yeah, soon."

They gave one another a fierce hug; then Meriwether hefted her carry-on over one shoulder and waved with her free hand as she took up the handle of her larger rolling bag. "Bye!" she called, following Dr. Knight through the revolving door and into the terminal.

They'd made their reservations sort of last minute, so they were seated apart from one another during all three flights. No matter, there was plenty of time to chat during the extensive layovers in both Dallas and New York. Thunderstorms kept them grounded in Dallas for close to three hours, which put them late for their original flight out of JFK. Meriwether was exceedingly thankful that her father was with her because he, being a well-seasoned traveler, knew just what to do to get a new flight scheduled.

Meriwether slept for most of the overseas flight and awoke feeling fuzzy, funky, and crumpled. It seemed like at least two days since she'd taken a shower. She rubbed her teeth with her finger and dug the sleep out of her eyes. Her hair was beyond help, but she did the best she could to smooth it with her hands, pulling it back into a bumpy pony-tail. Her upper body was sweaty from the blanket the flight attendant had brought her, but her left foot was near frozen from its too long placement in front of an air conditioning vent.

It was definitely not at her best that she exited the plane, her air legs buckling beneath her from lack of use, when whom other than Daniel Pleasant, looking ever so agreeable in clothes he'd only been wearing for a few hours, a lock of reddish gold hair falling across his forehead, freckled face split into a wide grin, chocolate brown eyes twinkling, stepped forward from the crowd to meet them.

"Yikes!" he exclaimed happily when he saw Meriwether.

"Yikes, yourself," growled Meriwether with a fake show of temper. She knew Daniel couldn't care less how she looked, and she was determined not to let him know how embarrassed she really was.

"Daniel!" boomed Dr. Knight looking only slightly worse for wear, "I wasn't expecting to see you! Have you been here long? I'm afraid we're a bit later than planned."

"Nah, Gran has her ways," smiled Daniel, shaking Dr. Knight's hand. "We found out about the delays, and we thought you might could use another strong arm at the airport." Daniel flexed his wiry biceps and continued, "I know how this one packs," with a nod to Meriwether.

Meriwether's eyes and mouth opened wide, "I do not over pack!"

Dr. Knight and Daniel shared a look that meant, *yeah right*.

It was now the 29th, a full day later than when they had left Sterling City. Daniel helped them with their luggage and they took the first coach to Oxford they could catch. Meriwether's stomach was grumbling. She would have enjoyed a leisurely breakfast somewhere, but they were very anxious to get home.

And although Meriwether was a bit jet lagged, she was no longer sleepy. The now familiar countryside between London and her father's home in Oxford beckoned to her. She felt revived and ready for whatever the Meriwethers might dish out.

"This came for you just the day before yesterday," Daniel was saying as he handed Dr. Knight a small brown envelope. Meriwether could not see whom the letter was from, but she noticed that the address was penned in all capital letters. "We would have sent it on, but we knew there wouldn't be time. I think it's about . . .," Daniel looked sideways at Meriwether, "you know what."

Dr. Knight nodded, removed a pair of reading glasses from his breast pocket, and slit the envelope with his finger.

Meriwether sat up straighter in her cushioned seat. She wasn't sure, but she felt like this must have something to do with the thing her father had been working on . . . the thing that would make her stay at Meriwether Manor at least bearable.

She was right.

She pierced Daniel with a steady gaze, but he wasn't falling for it. He kept his eyes on Dr. Knight, who finished reading the note quickly, folded it up, inserted the letter back into the envelope, and handed it back to Daniel. "It's all arranged," he said. "Do you have everything settled on your end?"

Daniel nodded. Meriwether had had enough.

"*What* is going on?" she demanded, fists balled up into little knots.

Daniel and her father both smiled. Daniel looked to Dr. Knight, the question in his eye. Dr. Knight held out his palm in a *go ahead* gesture.

"I'm going with you!" exclaimed Daniel. "To Hawkshead!"

Meriwether was stunned. "What?" she cried. "But . . . but how? I mean, what about school?"

Daniel shrugged, "School's not really my thing."

Meriwether eyed Daniel suspiciously, "What do you mean; school's not your thing?"

Daniel shrugged again, staring out the window at a passing field of dairy cows, "I just decided not to go on to the next level, that's all."

"Because of me?!!" screeched Meriwether. "Daniel, I can't let you . . . ."

"It's nothing to do with you!" Daniel cut her off hotly. "Look Meriwether, I don't need another sermon. I've heard it plenty from me mum and Gran."

Meriwether was taken aback. Daniel had never

snapped at her before. The heat rose in her face, and she stared out her window as well to avoid looking at Daniel. "What will you do?" she asked the window.

"Well, for the next month or so, I'll be helping the gardener at Meriwether Manor. Your dad set it up for me . . . but if you'd rather me not go . . . ."

"No!" Meriwether turned back to face Daniel. "I mean, of course I want you to! You have no idea how much better it makes me feel to think of you there with me . . . I just . . . Oh, I don't know . . . I mean, what will you do *in the long run*?" Meriwether tried to keep the accusation out of her voice. She was only twelve. She had no business telling Daniel what to do, but the idea of dropping out of school was anathema to her. She looked to her father for help.

He sighed, "Daniel has made up his mind. I think we must allow him to choose his own course, however vehemently we disagree."

They spent the rest of the ride in strained silence . . . something Meriwether had never experienced with Daniel. He'd crossed his arms and closed his eyes, but Meriwether knew he was not asleep. Meriwether also knew there was more to this story. She would not accept Daniel's quitting school, but she would wait for a more opportune time to needle the truth out of him.

By the time they arrived in Oxford, Meriwether had decided to play it like nothing had ever happened. Daniel, thankfully, was willing to go along. Dr. Knight felt like he needed to go straight to the Ashmolean; he wanted to check on the shipment of Egyptian antiques that had put his new assistant over the edge. Daniel and Meriwether took the luggage and went on to the house.

240 Abingdon Road hadn't changed a bit, other than the mums that now graced the planters on the front stoop instead of the summer's geraniums. Mrs. Doone met them at the door with a large hug for Meriwether and a pat for her grandson, "Ooh, and ye've grown a wee bit I think. Taller, don't you think, Daniel?"

Daniel shrugged noncommittally. "I'll just take these upstairs then," he said, hefting the suitcases up the narrow stairs.

As soon as Daniel was out of earshot, Mrs. Doone was pulling Meriwether across the faded kilim rug of the entry, past the stairwell, and into the small dining room that, unless you were actually sitting at the table, was standing room only. Mrs. Doone was so tiny that she and Meriwether were almost eye to eye, "I guess you've heard about Daniel, then," she whispered so heavily that her glasses fogged over.

Meriwether nodded, an empathetic grimace squinching her features. Mrs. Doone took off her glasses and wiped at them with a handkerchief she kept in her skirt pocket. Meriwether was uncomfortable to detect some moisture in the housekeeper's eyes.

"Don't know where we've gone wrong with that boy," she lamented, shaking her head of wispy white hair.

"There's nothing wrong with Daniel, Mrs. Doone," Meriwether said in a valiant effort to stick up for her friend. "Just give him some time . . . he'll come around."

"Aye, when he's married, has three young 'uns runnin' bouts, and strugglin' to bring home 20,000£ a year . . . then he'll come around. But by then it'll be too late!" predicted Mrs. Doone darkly.

Meriwether tried to picture this dire image of

Daniel's future, but she couldn't. Somehow, she knew that Daniel would be okay, and she said as much to Mrs. Doone. "I don't believe it! We'll work this thing out, Mrs. Doone. Don't you worry."

Mrs. Doone dabbed at the corners of her eyes with the handkerchief, then blew her nose into it loudly, "I do hope so, Meriwether. I do hope so."

They heard Daniel descending the stairs, whistling. Mrs. Doone pulled herself together quickly, drug Meriwether into the kitchen, and with a surprising show of strength, plopped her down at the table. She set down a mug of tea and a plate of scones in front of Meriwether just as Daniel entered.

Meriwether was reminded of her first visit to this kitchen and the interrupted conversation that she was sure had been about her. She smiled innocently at Daniel, "Scone?"

Chapter Four

After their mid morning snack, Meriwether and Daniel went for a walk through the nearby grounds of Christ Church College. Meriwether was pleased to note that she needed a jacket to shield her from the brisk wind that had blown up since breakfast.

They walked in silence for a while, each absorbed in his/her own thoughts. Meriwether drank in the beauty of the meadow, alive with the sights and sounds she had grown to love over the summer. Before them lay carpets of vividly green grass sewn with pebbled paths. Ancient canopies of trees, through which peeked similarly ancient glimpses of Oxford's towering spires, and romantic, curved bridges crossing small rivulets of the Isis beckoned the pair.

On the river, a team of young men swung their oars in rhythm to the call of their captain. Birds and squirrels chirped and chattered, "Faster, faster, faster!"

Students were everywhere. Classes were in full swing, and the crackle and excitement of university life was tangible in the air.

Again, Meriwether was troubled by Daniel's incredible decision. She would never understand it. She couldn't wait to someday find herself in a beautiful place like this . . . *learning* things . . . *becoming* something . . . *someone...*

"What's wrong?" Daniel asked suddenly, hands jammed in pants pockets.

"What do you mean?" she hedged.

Daniel shrugged, "You're frowning."

"Oh," Meriwether thought quickly, "just thinking about going to my grandparents'. They're not very nice people, you know."

"Yeah, you're dad told me a bit," he nodded. "Sounds like right snots to me . . . the way they treated your mum and all. Wonder why he wants you to go?"

It was Meriwether's turn to shrug, "I don't know." She looked up at Daniel, "I am glad you're going with me."

Daniel smiled a brilliant smile that warmed Meriwether better than any cup of hot chocolate could possibly have done. "It's a secret; you know. . . my being there."

Meriwether was confused, "But I thought Dad set it up with the gardener? He said . . ."

"Yeah, he set it up with the gardener . . . Mr. Greene . . . but Mr. and Mrs. Meriwether don't know anything about it," explained Daniel.

"You mean, this *Mr. Greene* is able to hire help without consulting them?" Meriwether squinted suspiciously.

"Guess so. He agreed to have me, didn't he?" Meriwether nodded, chewing the inside of her lip. "He's picking us up from the train station. You'll stay in the big house with your grandparents, and I'll stay in the gardener's cottage with Greene."

Meriwether thought about that for a moment, then

Daniel continued, "Don't know how much we'll actually get to speak or anything. You'll probably have to act like you don't know me if your grandparents are around . . . and then you'll have your *tutor*," his face puckered up, just like he'd put a nasty spoonful of something into his mouth, "so it depends on how much you can get away with . . . but at least I'll be, you know, a friendly face . . . there if you get into any trouble."

"Is that what my dad said?" shot Meriwether.

Daniel grinned, "Well your track record is 0 for 2."

Meriwether sniffed, "I prefer to think of it as 2 and 0."

Daniel shrugged, "You say tomato, I say tom*ah*to."

Chapter Five

Meriwether tried hard not to get anything dirty over the next two days so that Mrs. Doone wouldn't have to do much washing, but laundry was inevitable. Early Sunday evening, as a misty dusk settled over the venerable city, Meriwether helped Mrs. Doone fold clothes still warm from the dryer as her father paced nervously from one end of the room to the next.

A cheery fire crackled in the grate, and the golden gilt titles of a hundred books winked merrily at Meriwether. Meriwether's favorite picture, the one of her mother laughing in the grass along the banks of the Isis, smiled at her from Dr. Knight's leather topped desk. A set of Russian nesting dolls, just like the ones her father had sent her for her third birthday, shared space with the books, and two Ali-Babba oil lamps, flanking either side of the mantle, sat astride the bronzed figure of a ferocious Chinese lion. It was all so irresistibly homey -- except for the pacing part -- that Meriwether felt herself hoping against hope that something . . . anything might happen to prevent her having to leave tomorrow morning.

Dr. Knight was clearly nervous.

Meriwether kept looking up at him expectantly, waiting for him to say, "Never mind. You're not going."

But he never did. Instead, Mrs. Doone in her lilting native Welsh said, "Tell us about the shipment from Egypt, then."

The lines of worry were immediately erased from his face as Dr. Knight stopped pacing and sat down opposite them in a faded, cushy armchair. "Marvelous find, actually," he began, the familiar fever burning bright in his eyes. "From a new tomb . . . and it's been ages since they've found a new tomb. We're very lucky that Dr. Ahmed is on our payroll . . . he's the one who discovered it. Jean's been up to her eyeballs in objects that needed cleaning and classifying. A bit beyond her . . . but it's a learning curve . . . to be thrown out of your element like that. I think she's done quite nicely for a student... couldn't have expected anything more."

"And did you tell her, then?" asked Mrs. Doone.

Dr. Knight frowned in genuine confusion, "Tell her what?"

Mrs. Doone let escape a small puff of air from the back of her throat, "*Tell her* that she's done a good job . . . that you're pleased with her work . . . ."

"Oh." Obviously he hadn't.

"Of course it's not all been smooth sailing, he continued." "Some of the objects we were to receive have been lost in transit . . . that is to say . . . we don't have everything that's on the list."

"The list?" wondered Meriwether.

"Ahmed sent a packing list detailing the contents of the crates he shipped. We've not found all of the objects. Probably a clerical error . . . we just need to compare notes," Dr. Knight dissed the subject with a shrug.

This was really very interesting. Meriwether had always been enthralled with ancient Egypt. Dr. Knight had sent her a sandstone figurine of the Egyptian god Ra for her fifth birthday. Grandmother had clicked her tongue and put it away without ceremony, but the strange little idol had sparked something in Meriwether. She had since devoured everything she could get her hands on about Egypt and was quite familiar with many of the pharaohs and their dynasties. "Whose tomb do they think it was?"

"Very interesting you should ask," Dr. Knight said with a gleam in his eye. "I'll have to get back to you on that one." His jaw closed with a snap, and Meriwether knew she would have to accept this cryptic response . . . *darn it!*

"Best be off to bed with ye', Meriwether," said Mrs. Doone, nodding at the clock on the bookshelf. "You've an early morning of it."

Early didn't quite cut it, as far as Meriwether was concerned. Mrs. Meriwether had said she would expect Meriwether on the morning train from Oxford. That morning train arrived in Hawkshead at 10:00 a.m. -- but it *left* at 4:00 a.m. That meant getting up close to 3:00, at the very latest. Meriwether thought it might be better not to go to bed at all.

She said her goodnights and trudged up the stairs to her room, the one Mrs. Doone had fixed up for her earlier that summer. The walls were papered in a cheery pink and white stripe. A whitewashed iron bed took up most of the room, and if you were sitting on the bed, a mirrored armoire was on your right, a writing desk on your left. If you sat at the desk, you could look out the window onto Abingdon Road, one of Oxford's busiest thoroughfares. Meriwether loved this room as much as she loved her large, clean-lined, shades of blue room at home in Texas.

Meriwether didn't feel tired, so she lingered over her bedtime routine. She carefully laid out her clothes for the morning: black leggings and a soft, swingy tunic style sweater that came almost to her knees. She wanted to look good when she met her mother's family, but she also wanted to be comfortable on the train.

She brushed her hair slowly, savoring the tingle of the bristles against her scalp, and thought over her morning's trip to St. Mary's, Iffley, with Mrs. Doone. She was practically a hero there now, her discovery having brought in a rush of new tourism to the ancient little parish. Suffice it to say, the organization of bake sales was no longer necessary.

Reverend March and his wife Virginia had given them a heart stopping ride home and had stayed for Sunday lunch. Over roast beef, potatoes, and carrots, Dr. Knight and Meriwether told them their story of finding the pterosaur fossil in the cave back in Texas. When Dr. Knight mentioned Lainey Mason his eyes twinkled, and Rev. March's blue eyes twinkled happily in return. He and Dr. Knight had been friends for a long time.

Meriwether sighed. It had been a good day.

She took some stationery from her desk and began a letter to Holly -- Chapter one. She'd write more later and send it on from Hawkshead. *Hawkshead* . . . the very name sent shivers up her spine. It sounded cold . . . severe . . . cruel even. Once again, she was glad she wouldn't be alone.

By now, she was getting sleepy. She snuggled deep under the down comforter and turned out the art glass bedside lamp. She tried to pray, but her thoughts all jumbled together into a garble of wordless emotion. She trusted that God knew what she meant and whispered, "Amen," anyway.

Before she knew it, her father was knocking on her door. "Time to get up, Meriwether," he murmured, his voice still thick from sleep. He left the door ajar, and light from the hall reached into her room.

I can't do it, thought Meriwether, but she held her breath and swung her legs out of bed anyway. The worst was over, and she began the task of getting ready, glad she'd already decided what to wear the night before . . . . What was she talking about? . . . . It was *still* night!

A few short minutes later, dressed and half awake, Meriwether stumbled down the stairs to be handed a thermos of sweet hot tea and hugged by Mrs. Doone. She was still wrapped in her house coat and looked so tiny and fragile that Meriwether was again surprised at the strength of her bony embrace.

"You'll take care of my Daniel, then," she said shakily, tears in her eyes. Meriwether nodded, trying not to cry. Gathering herself, Mrs. Doone handed Meriwether and her father their coats as she pushed them out the front door, "Hurry along . . . cab's waiting, but the train won't!"

The morning was dark . . . and cold! Meriwether quickly shrugged into her new green wool duffle as Dr. Knight and the taxi driver loaded her bags into the boot of the little car. As Meriwether climbed into the taxi, she took one last, longing look at #240 Abingdon Road. She saw Mrs. Doone peering out the curtains of her father's study, clutching at the neck of her robe with one hand, the other against the glass in a final, plaintive wave.

Meriwether pressed her own palm against the

window of the cab and swiveled in the back seat to watch Mrs. Doone grow smaller . . . and smaller . . . and smaller. The cab skirted through the sleeping city and back into an area of Oxford that Meriwether was not familiar with. She knew they were picking up Daniel and stared out her window, eager to get a glimpse of the home he shared with his mother.

Meriwether's heart dropped as the taxi rolled to a stop outside a nondescript row of gray and dilapidated flats.

Dr. Knight got out to knock on the front door -- Meriwether thought she knew the one . . . fiery magenta, even in the early morning gloom -- but before he could get there Daniel burst through the door Meriwether had picked out and tripped lightly down the steps, one bulging satchel thrown over his shoulder.

He threw the satchel in with Meriwether's luggage and, grinning like a cat, slid in beside her in the backseat. Dr. Knight climbed in front with the cabbie, and they were off.

They got there just in time. Dr. Knight bade them a hasty goodbye, crushing Meriwether with a giant bear hug . . . a handshake and pat on the back for Daniel. No one said much. The emotions were much too high. Dr. Knight remembered the tin of muffins Mrs. Doone had sent and handed them off to Daniel as they boarded the train.

"Goodbye!" he called, waving as the train pulled out of the station, "Goodbye!"

Meriwether watched her father disappear, much as she had Mrs. Doone. Smaller, he dropped his arm and his shoulders stooped. Smaller still, he collapsed onto a nearby bench; his head fell into his hands . . . . He was gone.

    Meriwether turned to look at Daniel, wondering if he'd seen what she just had. He hadn't. They sat facing one another on the train; Meriwether was looking back, Daniel was looking forward. Meriwether could see the excitement on his face, and she realized how ready he was to get away from what had become so familiar to him. If he had any trepidation at all about leaving school, he didn't show it.

    Daniel peeled the lid off the tin and the two shared some of Mrs. Doone's still warm muffins. Night covered them like a cloak, and so, bellies full, they each nodded off to sleep, lulled by the gentle lurch and sway of the coach.

    On and on they went. It seemed like they stopped at every village they came to.

    People got on; people got off.

    This starting and stopping didn't seem to bother Daniel. He slept on, mouth slightly agape, his tweedy brown cap pulled down over his eyes. Meriwether, on the other hand, woke up each time. She finally gave up and decided to read some of the novel Miss Fisher had assigned her English class. She took out her highlighter. Grandmother had bought Meriwether her own copy so that she could mark passages that stood out to her in the book -- things she thought might be important later, that she could use in her essay, or that might show up on a test.

    Holly would always roll her eyes whenever she saw Meriwether doing this. But who was always calling whom -- frantic -- the night before the essay was due -- wondering where did it say this . . . or where did it say that? The thought of Holly made Meriwether smile, and then it made her frown, and then she realized she had read an entire page without absorbing a bit of it. Sighing, she began again at the top of the page, highlighter poised and at the ready, determined to pay attention to her task.

Daniel stirred, then stretched, then grinned. Meriwether put her book away . . . study time was over.

At 10:00 sharp the train stopped in front of the Hawkshead station. Meriwether and Daniel were stretching their legs, waiting in front of the doors when they opened. Daniel had kept his satchel with him, but they had to locate Meriwether's luggage. They saw a blue uniformed man hefting something red from a compartment underneath the passenger car and walked over to gather her things.

As they had traveled north through England, Meriwether had noticed a definite change in the scenery that surrounded them. This area, known as the Lake District, was darker, wilder . . . more dramatic than the gently rolling hills and picture card vistas of Oxfordshire and the Cotswolds.

From where she was standing, however, Meriwether could see neither hill nor vale -- only people bustling about, in a hurry to go here or there, babies crying, trains arriving and departing, and men in their blue uniforms making sure everything ran like clockwork.

After collecting her luggage, Meriwether and Daniel did not know what to do. They knew that Mr. Greene was supposed to meet them at the station and take them on to Meriwether Manor, but they didn't know what Mr. Greene looked like . . . and he didn't know them. Meriwether kept her eyes out sharp for an older gentleman who seemed to be looking for someone.

When she saw him walking toward them it was

instant recognition. She didn't need anyone to tell her. This thin, weather beaten man with eyes almost completely hidden behind folds of sagging skin and a stubble of white whiskers on his jowly face was their Mr. Greene.

She began walking to meet him, a red valise in each hand. They stopped about two feet short of collision. It was if they had always known one another.

Chapter Six

Mr. Greene tipped his hat, "Hallo, ...Let me take them bags for ye."

"Thank you, Mr. Greene," smiled Meriwether.

"Call me Jacob," he smiled back, showing rows of small, tobacco stained teeth.

Meriwether heard Daniel clear his throat politely behind her, "Oh, Jacob, this is Daniel, Daniel Pleasant."

Daniel stepped forward and held out his hand, "Hello, sir."

Mr. Greene enveloped Daniel's hand in what must have been an iron grip. Daniel gritted his teeth into a toothy grin. Meriwether could tell by his eyes that it hurt, but he didn't flinch. Apparently, Mr. Greene was impressed because he growled, "Aye, ye're a strong lad, jis' like Dr. Knight said. I hope ye're not afraid a hard work."

"No, sir," said Daniel, flexing his fingers to make sure they still worked.

Mr. Greene led them to a small, very low to the ground pick-up. It was banana yellow and reminded Meriwether of the American El Camino you still saw from time to time. He had lain a tarp down in the bed of the truck and placed Meriwether's luggage carefully upon it. He then pulled the remainder of the tarp over her bags and secured the ends with some large rocks he carried in the back of his truck.

He eyed Daniel, "Throw it in the back, boy. There's not enough room up front."

Daniel obeyed, and they all scrambled into the bench seat, Meriwether squashed in the middle. She frowned to herself. Why was Jacob being so nice to her and so gruff with Daniel? She didn't think he was patronizing her. No, she had felt an instant connection with the old man . . . almost like she *remembered* him . . . but that was impossible. As far as she knew, even as a baby, she had never been to Meriwether Manor.

Daniel looked nonplussed and a little pale as they left the main road and traveled treacherously along a narrow, winding one. Meriwether wondered what he was thinking . . . but now was not the time to ask.

They seemed to be going up. Looking across Mr. Greene and out the driver's side window, Meriwether could see a glassy black lake, the dark trees of the wood reflected in its mirrored surface. Higher and higher they climbed, then right onto a graveled path marked with a high stone wall and scrolled iron gate, almost completely camouflaged by the dense vegetation that grew up around it.

"This be the beginnin' o' the grounds," growled Jacob, and Meriwether let out a gasp. Through a formal colonnade of mature trees, Meriwether could just glimpse the many gables and tended gardens of Meriwether Manor.

Meriwether chanced a glance at Daniel. His brown eyes were huge in his face as they approached some hairy, reddish deer foraging not far from the path. The deer were not afraid of the truck and as it passed, continued to graze contentedly at the velvet covering of green that stretched from tree to tree.

They were getting closer, and Meriwether could see the pitch of the roof as it rose and fell, rose and fell, a dozen chimney pots jutting up against the sky. Massive wooden doors marked the landing, and a hundred mullioned windows of every size and shape broke the formidable brick and stone facade. Daniel whistled under his breath.

Before they got to the main house, Mr. Greene pulled off in front of a low, thatched, rain-stained cottage, hedged neatly by an orchard that gave it privacy from the manor. It was the gardener's cottage, and not exactly what Meriwether would call cheery, but it was tidy and close. She could imagine Daniel here with Mr. Greene, eating supper and sitting around the fire at night after a long day's work. Maybe she could sneak down sometimes and share a cup of tea.

A few chickens scratched in the yard and a big white cat lazed on the walk in front of the door. Meriwether smiled to herself; it looked just like a painting.

"Daniel, you take ye'r things in and wait for me. I'll take the miss up to the big house, then we'll have us a spot o' lunch an' get to work . . . and remember you two," he pierced them both with his hang dog eyes, "ye' don' know one another . . . so doan'a be speakin' unless ye're sure's ye're alone."

Meriwether and Daniel nodded solemnly. "See ya around," waved Daniel as he climbed out of the truck and headed up the flagstone walk. He stepped over the lounging cat, who batted at his pants leg playfully, got up, and followed him inside.

"See ya!" Meriwether's heart leapt up in her chest.

This was it.

Jacob's wheels crunched on the fine gravel that made up the drive. Meriwether climbed out and in a moment of madness, was tempted to kick up a shower of it with the toe of her ballet flat, ruining the perfection of the line that separated gravel bed from green grass lawn. She was able to resist, and the moment passed -- no damage done.

Jacob went around to the back of the pick-up to get her things and motioned with his head for Meriwether to go ahead. Meriwether took a deep breath and, feeling very small, began to slowly climb the great stone steps. She raised her hand to the lion's head knocker, but before she'd even touched it the door was opened by a young woman in black and white servant's dress. Her strawberry blonde hair was pulled back into a low knot. She had an easy, open face, and a squarish fringe of bangs framed large gray eyes. Flashing a quick smile she said, "Hallo. This way. Mrs. Meriwether is expectin' ye."

As the girl turned, Meriwether took in her surroundings. A grand staircase dominated the entry. To her right stood a heavy marble topped table and an ornate, gold framed mirror. At their feet lay a worn tiger skin rug, the poor beast's face sunken and shriveled against the cut stone floor. A busy William Morris print wallpaper of brown and gold floribunda covered the walls, and a massive chandelier, unlit, hung heavily above. Meriwether ducked involuntarily as they walked under it.

She followed the girl into a room that looked as if it belonged to a different house entirely, tastefully decorated in varying hues of gray, blue, and white. Sunlight streamed through the window illuminating a woman, Meriwether assumed it must be her grandmother, at a ladies writing desk, her back to them. The servant girl did not say anything. They stood on the threshold of the room and waited as Mrs. Meriwether, without rush, completed whatever it was that she was doing.

"Thank you, Mary. That will be all," the woman said, rising.

Mary curtsied to her mistress's back and fairly bustled from the room. Her eyes sought Meriwether's as she left. What was in that enigmatic look?

Pity?

Fear?

Meriwether dug her fingernail into her thumb and forced her mother's image into her brain. *She* had grown up here. This woman turning about so cooly had been *her* mother. Meriwether shook her head. Somehow it didn't fit.

She was a small woman, thin as a rail, with bony hands and neck. Her steel gray hair was curled and swept becomingly back from her face, but it did little to soften the sharpness of her beakish nose and jawline. Quick, beady eyes pierced Meriwether. There was something very birdlike about her.

Wasn't the modern bird supposed to be a descendant of the dinosaur? Meriwether could see it . . . *vestiges of the velociraptor ...* "Hello, Meriwether. Come here, and let me have a look at you," a disagreeable voice issuing a disagreeable command.

Fingernail still in her thumb, giving her something to concentrate on, Meriwether made herself walk toward her grandmother.

Mrs. Meriwether appraised her granddaughter as she might a domesticated animal she was prepared to buy. The old woman who walked around Meriwether in a wide circle was dressed conservatively in a herringbone skirt suit of heathered blue. Low black pumps covered her small feet, and a circular pin with a large opal in the middle graced her lapel.

Next to her grandmother, Meriwether's bright, swingy sweater and black tights suddenly felt garishly Bohemian, more at home in the eclectic entry than in this pale washed room; clearly Mrs. Meriwether's domain. She wished she had worn one of her more demure Sunday skirts, but it was too late now.

After revolving about her completely, Mrs. Meriwether stopped. Standing back, she crossed one arm in front of her body and rested the other elbow in the hand at her waist. Her open palm covered the corner of her mouth as she looked Meriwether up and down in open assessment.

Meriwether fidgeted nervously with the soft hem of her sweater. How long could this go on?

"Jacob will take your things to your room and Mary will help you unpack. I hope you've brought some things suitable for our Sunday service. If not, we'll have to arrange a trip in to Thorpe's tomorrow," she rattled. Then, remembering her manners, "I trust you've had a pleasant journey?"

"Yes ma'am. Thank you," Meriwether hadn't forgotten hers. She smiled to herself, thinking *yes, I did have a pleasant journey . . . Pleasant, Daniel Pleasant.*

Mrs. Meriwether nodded, "Very well." She took a small silver bell from her waist pocket and jangled it, "I must finish my correspondence, but Mary will see you to your room. Luncheon is at noon, sharp. It's a lovely day, so I think we'll eat out on the veranda, through these doors." Mrs. Meriwether indicated French doors leading to an open air patio. Meriwether could see English ivy climbing the walls and an iron filigree table and chairs tucked into a leafy corner.

"You may tour the grounds until then, but I do expect you to wash up before we eat." And with that, Mrs. Meriwether turned around and sat back down at her desk. She picked up her pen and began to scribble away.

A dismissal.

Meriwether stood there dumbly, her heart like a block of ice.

She felt a tap on her shoulder. Turning around, she found Mary, tip-toeing and motioning with her finger for Meriwether to follow.

Up the staircase they went. At the first landing they took a left and passed a series of closed doors. Meriwether counted them as they passed by. One, two, three, four, five, six . . . sixth door on the right . . . this was her room. Mary opened the door and held it open for Meriwether to pass through. Another room like the tiger's den.

Old red and gold Oriental carpets covered stretches of stone, and a gleaming antique dresser sat opposite an enormous four poster dressed luxuriously in layers of cream bedding, a silk brocade throw slung artfully across the foot of the bed. One expansive, mullioned window dominated the far wall, and from it Meriwether could see green grass leading to a forest of trees, bits of blue sky, and a glimpse of the lake they had passed on their way up.

A black and white photograph of a child walking and holding a man's hand in a garden stood as lone adornment on the dresser, and it drew Meriwether's gaze like a spotlight. For of course she thought she knew who this child must be.

Could this have been *her* room?

Meriwether did hope so.

"Whot do ye think?" asked Mary, proudly.

"It's a beautiful room. Thank you," answered Meriwether. She wanted to say, *Was it my mother's?*, but Mary was much too young to have known Felicia. In fact, Meriwether wouldn't put her a day over 19. That would have made Mary eight years old when Felicia died, and less than that when she'd left home for Oxford. She needed to find someone older. Maybe Jacob?

Mary smiled, pleased. "I clean it meself, and if ye need anythin', just call. I'm always about."

Meriwether liked the way Mary talked. It was fun just to stand there and listen to her. If she'd grown up here instead of in Texas, would she sound like Mary . . . or Mrs. Meriwether? Mrs. Meriwether's speech was very precise and came from the back of her throat. Meriwether found the harsh tone, not the accent, offensive.

Mary was still waiting, and Meriwether didn't know what to say. She was looking at Meriwether expectantly . . . surely she wasn't waiting for a tip?

"I'm supposed to help ye unpack. Mrs. Meriwether says so," helped Mary.

"Oh, okay," Meriwether blushed in spite of herself. This was all a little much. She felt like a character from one of the books she was always reading. She looked around for her suitcases and, sure enough, there they were, stacked neatly beside the bed. *How did Jacob get these up here without making any noise?*, she wondered. Shrugging to herself, she walked over and hefted the biggest of the bags onto the bed. She began laying out the clothes as Mary took them and either hung them up or stowed them in the dresser. In no time at all they were finished.

"All settled then?" smiled Mary, dusting her hands on her apron.

Meriwether nodded, "Yes. Thank you for helping me, Mary."

Mary's eyes widened in surprise and two spots of color formed high on her full cheeks. She did a funny little curtsy and bolted from the room.

Meriwether was dying to get out and have a look around, but it was already past 11:00, and lunch was scheduled for noon. Besides, she was very tired. Anxiety mixed with too little sleep had left her feeling achy and drained. The high bed and its layers of down called to her. She would just take a little nap . . . .

Chapter Seven

Daniel paced the worn stone floor of the cottage waiting for Mr. Greene to get back and set him to work. He hadn't come all this way to pet cats and sit in front of the fire.

Through the kitchen window and a gap in Greene's orchard, Daniel could just see Meriwether Manor. It was impressive, but it made him shiver to look at it. He felt sorry for Meriwether, there all alone.

Well, he was here to protect her . . . or at least that's the way he looked at it. He stopped pacing and tried to pass some good energy, some positive thoughts on to Meriwether, like his mum was always going on about -- not that he believed in any of that mumbo jumbo . . . but it couldn't hurt, right?

It hadn't taken long to explore Greene's compact cottage. Living room, kitchen, two tiny bedrooms, Daniel had thrown his satchel onto the chenille bedspread in the room that was obviously unoccupied. If Daniel had been a little bit more curious, a little more like Meriwether, he might have taken to rifling through drawers and medicine cabinets out of boredom . . . but the thought never even occurred to him.

Mid-stride, Daniel heard the impatient bleep! bleep!

of Mr. Greene's horn. Careful not to trip over the cat that dogged his heels, Daniel went out to meet the old man. Greene motioned with his head for Daniel to get in.

"Day's a wastin'," he growled.

So much for lunch.

Chapter Eight

Knock, knock, knock, " Meriwether!" Knock, knock, knock, " Meriwether!" Mary opened the door and flitted over to the bed with its apparently comatose occupant. She shook the figure with both hands, " MERIWETHER!"

Meriwether opened her eyes, groggily, "Wha . . .?"

"Ye'r late fer luncheon with Mrs. Meriwether! She's settin' on the veranda waitin' for ye . . . an' she doesn't like to be kept waitin'!"

Meriwether bolted out of bed and grabbed the brush that was sitting on the bureau. *Thank goodness Mary had helped her unpack!* She quickly raked the bristles through her hair that had, of course, tangled while she slept. Mary fetched her a wet rag and she wiped her face and hands with it gratefully. She tumbled down the stairs in a mad dash, only slowing as she reached Mrs. Meriwether's blue room.

Through the French doors, she could see Mrs. Meriwether waiting for her at the carefully laid table. Her foot tapped in annoyance, and her mouth was drawn into a sharp line.

With a deep breath, Meriwether opened the doors, crossed the patio, and took her seat across from her grandmother. "I'm sorry I'm late," she apologized.

Mrs. Meriwether arched an eyebrow, removed the cloth napkin in front of her, and smoothed it across her lap. A plump woman with graying hair escaping from her caplet appeared from nowhere. In her hands were two plates filled with a fresh greens salad and sandwich wedge on whole grain.

"Thank you, Martha," said Mrs. Meriwether as she set the plates in front of them.

Martha nodded, turned around, and disappeared behind a door half hidden in ivy. Meriwether supposed it must lead to the kitchen. Had Martha winked at her when Mrs. Meriwether wasn't looking?

The two ate in silence. The chicken salad sandwich had sprouts in it, which Meriwether did not particularly care for, but she didn't dare pick them out. As they finished, Martha reappeared with a plate of small cookies.

"Mrs. Meriwether doesn't take sweets, but I thought the might like to try me lime meltaways," Martha chattered as she removed Meriwether's dinner plate and replaced it with the cookie laden one. "One o' Col. Meriwether's favorites . . . an' now 'e can't even eat 'em!" Tears gathered in her eyes, and she hastily wiped at them with a handkerchief from her pocket. "I'm sorry, ma'am," she said to Mrs. Meriwether.

"That will be all, Martha," replied Mrs. Meriwether frostily.

"Thank you, Mrs. . . ?" Meriwether felt funny calling this older woman by her given name.

Martha beamed, "Mrs. Cook . . . Martha Cook . . . that's me name!"

Meriwether began again, "Thank you, Mrs. Cook. The cookies are delicious!" Meriwether made a mental note to catch Mrs. Cook alone and request *no more sprouts, please*.

Martha nodded to them both, and with a, "Ma'am," for Mrs. Meriwether and a -- *yes, this time it was definitely a wink* -- for Meriwether, Mrs. Cook took her exit.

Meriwether nibbled the delicate little tea cookies that did, indeed, melt in her mouth. Mrs. Meriwether watched her for some time. It was uncomfortable, but at least the business of eating gave her something to do.

Finally, Mrs. Meriwether spoke. "You look very much like your mother."

Meriwether was instantly on guard. She wanted to say all sorts of things like *and you would have known that if you'd ever taken the trouble to get to know me* **or** *my mother, huh? . . . how about* **your daughter***? . . . the one you cut out of your life completely because you didn't approve of my dad?* Biting her tongue was getting to be great exercise.

Meriwether decided to bait the waters, "But my hair is dark, like my dad's."

Mrs. Meriwether didn't bite. "Obviously."

"Mary tells me you have brought proper clothing. I plan to inspect your closet myself, but if all is in order, I think we can rule out the trip to Thorpe's tomorrow. Regardless, I've some business in town, and you are welcome to accompany me if you'd like. I think you would enjoy Hawkshead."

Was the woman trying? It was hard to tell. Meriwether thought quickly. If she didn't go to Hawkshead, she could spend the day with Daniel. Sure, he'd be working . . . but she could help. And manual labor at Daniel's side was more enticing than an afternoon with prickly Mrs. Meriwether -- any day of the week! Still, she didn't feel like she could politely refuse, and Grandmother had raised her well.

"That would be nice. Thank you," *spit and vinegar*.

"Very well then. It's settled. We dress for dinner in this house. I will expect you promptly at 7:00 in the dining room. Col. Meriwether plans to join us if he is up to it, so it is very important that you are on time. We'll leave for Hawkshead at 8:30. I take breakfast in my room, but Martha will fix you something in the kitchen whenever you come down." She stopped abruptly, the unspoken *any questions?* hanging in the air.

Meriwether nodded, "Yes, ma'am."

Mrs. Meriwether rose. "Enjoy your afternoon," she said, leaving Meriwether with her cookies.

It was a cool, crisp, sunny afternoon -- just the sort Meriwether liked best -- so, determined not to let Mrs. Meriwether rain on her parade, Meriwether decided to go exploring. She'd give herself a few hours to check the place out; then she would bathe, work on some of her lessons, and get ready for dinner. Armed with her plan for the day, Meriwether put a few cookies in the pocket of her sweater, in case she got hungry later, and made a path through the grass toward the back of the house.

The manor was huge. *There must be a hundred rooms in this place*, thought Meriwether, anticipating the inside job she planned to carry out in the near future. Who knew what secrets a good search might turn up?

At the rear of the house spread a formal English garden. Meriwether imagined it at its full glory, but it was no less lovely now. A few late roses clung to their splintery stalks. In their midst, a young Grecian girl, hair piled high, plump shoulders bare, reached out to touch the blossoms that she could not see.

A reflecting pool anchored the garden, and on its rim sat a snow white cat. Was it the same one Meriwether had seen at Mr. Greene's? Meriwether walked slowly to the pool, so as not to startle the cat. As she got closer, she could see what he was doing . . . watching the exceptionally large goldfish that swam in the water. Meriwether's approach disturbed the fish, which flitted over to the far side of the pool. The cat looked up at Meriwether with large green eyes. "Thanks, thanks a lot," those eyes spoke, clear as day.

"Sorry," Meriwether said out loud.

She sat down on the edge of the pool and rubbed the cat's ears. His purr vibrated like a small engine, and he began crossing over her lap and under her arm, rubbing himself all over her.

She sneezed.

Affronted, the cat jumped down and sauntered across the grass, back toward the house.

"I'm allergic!" Meriwether called after him in vain. She watched the swishing white tail until it disappeared, shrugged, and followed a gravel path until it disappeared into the trees.

The sunlight was immediately obliterated, and in the shadows hung a dampness that permeated what suddenly seemed a very thin sweater. Meriwether shivered and wished she had grabbed a jacket . . . or at least changed her shoes. She would have to step lightly to avoid ruining her slippers, and she wore them with just about everything!

From her bedroom window, Meriwether had seen a glimpse of the lake, Blelham Tarn she thought it was, based on her scanty research into the area. She wanted to make it to the other side of these trees to see if she could get a better look at it.

On into the forest she forged, only peripherally aware that she was getting further and further away from the house, and that the terrain was getting rougher and rougher.

The ground began to slope as Meriwether picked her way down some rocky escarpments. The wood was unnaturally silent, as if all its inhabitants were watching, waiting to see what this intruder was up to. Through a break in the trees, Meriwether could see a cliff side clearing. She rushed toward the crag and looked down, triumphant, upon Blelham Tarn.

The view was breathtaking and terrifying all at once. A strong sensation of vertigo shot up from her belly and turned her head fuzzy. Meriwether stepped back from the edge. Her ankle gave way beneath her and she came down hard on the mossy ground. Blood oozed from a gash in her head as her vision clouded and her eyelids closed. Then darkness... the eyes in the forest lingered upon the fallen girl, yet she did not get up.

Chapter Nine

Daniel was starving.

After mulching some of the gardens, he and Mr. Greene had worked all afternoon pruning trees in the orchard that separated Greene's cottage from the manor house. Lunch had consisted of sardines from a can and saltines that the gardener kept in his truck. Daniel had eaten them to be polite . . . and because he was hungry . . . but it hadn't been nearly enough to fill the growing boy, and the fishy taste of the sardines had stayed in his mouth all afternoon.

I bet Meriwether had a nice enough lunch, he thought mutinously.

It was close to dark. The little fire Greene had going in his grate had gone out, and an empty sort of chill filled the little cottage. "Get the fire a goin', kindlin's in the basket, an' I'll start us a pot o' soup," said Greene.

Soup! He'd do anything for some soup. Daniel hurried to his task, the cat at his heels wailing mournfully.

"Shut yer yowlin', Artemis!" Greene hollered good-naturedly. "Yer dinner's a comin'."

Daniel heard Greene set the cat's bowl down on the kitchen floor, so he knew that Artemis must have heard it too. But still, the cat did not leave Daniel's side -- meowing for all the world like he was trying to tell him something.

Well, Daniel didn't speak cat, and he wasn't in the mood to play detective. His arms ached already, and he knew they'd hurt worse tomorrow.

The fire smoked and caught; delicate orange flames licking up from the twigs and bits of straw. Daniel lay on his back with his hands behind his head and closed his eyes. The thin cotton rug felt like bliss to his overtired limbs. Artemis leapt on his chest and dug his claws through Daniel's shirt, "Maooo!"

"Oww! . . . you crazy cat!" Daniel yelled, sitting straight up and throwing Artemis off him. "What'd you do that for?"

Artemis gave him a withering look and retreated to the top of a cupboard from which he continued his resounding lament. Mr. Greene, shirt sleeves rolled up past his elbows, an onion in one hand, a large and very sharp knife in the other, walked out from the kitchen, "What in the name o' heaven's goin' on in here?"

"You're cat's insane . . . that's what's goin' on!" muttered Daniel as he looked down his shirt and counted cat scratches. They were already starting to itch.

Artemis turned to Mr. Greene, "Maooooo."

Mr. Greene eyed the cat, "Well, he likes ye . . . that's not the problem. Seen 'im followin' at yer heels like a lovesick puppy ever since ye got here. I think he's tryin' a tell us somethin'."

"Meow," replied Artemis. Finally, he was getting somewhere. In one graceful leap, Artemis was down from the cupboard. "Meow," he said again, looking back at the humans and swishing his tail . . . just in case they still didn't get it.

Jacob set the onion and the knife down on the sideboard, and then on second thought, picked the knife back up and stuck the blade through his belt. "Come on, boy."

"But what about the soup?" wailed Daniel.

"Soup can wait," growled Jacob, and he was out the door following the cat, a reluctant Daniel in his wake.

Plink! Plink! . . . Plink! Plink! Meriwether brushed her face . . . something cold . . . *rain!* . . . and something warm . . . *blood?*

Her fingers traced the gash, which was mostly clotted over by now, and tried to think where she was. Her eyes weren't doing her much good. It was dark . . . and drizzling . . . so she must be outside. She remembered a cat by a pool, . . . a gravel path, . . . trees, a cliff, a lake.

Realizing that her ankle was killing her, she pieced it all together. She must have tripped and fallen when she'd backed away from the precipice. Rolling to her side, she used her elbow to prop herself up. Her ankle was definitely swollen; that much was obvious . . . but could she put any weight on it?

Keeping her bad ankle straight out in front of her, Meriwether used the rock her head had hit to balance herself into a standing position. She gingerly put her foot down on the slippery ground . . . *ouch! Ouch, ouch, ouch!* And for the first time, Meriwether felt afraid.

No one knew where she was. She couldn't walk. Her head was swimming, and she was afraid she was going to pass out again. If she tried hopping in this rain, she was bound to trip and fall and hurt herself even worse.

So what now?

Deep breaths, she told herself.

A little bit of yoga breathing and a few whispered prayers later, Meriwether felt braver . . . calmer. She remembered the cookies in her pocket and sat down on the rock to eat them. They were a little mushed and fuzzy from her sweater, but they were still delicious. Meriwether realized how hungry she was, and then she remembered that she was supposed to meet her grandparents for dinner, washed and dressed, at 7:00 sharp.

She looked down at the fluorescent watch she wore: 6:55. She'd never make it. Even worse, this meant that nobody had even missed her yet. She sighed, slid down to the muddy ground and leaned against the rock. She pulled the sweater over the top of her head to shield her face from the light rain -- and waited.

Her breath on her own body helped to keep her warm, and Meriwether could feel the hair framing her face curling into tight ringlets. She focused on staying calm, straining for any sound in the dark that might mean that help was on its way.

And then, from inside the blind cocoon of her sweater, Meriwether sensed that someone -- or something -- was watching her. But surely no one was out here with her? If they were, they'd help her, right?

What was that?

A rustle in the trees, the crack of a fallen branch . . . . Meriwether pulled the sweater down and stared wildly into the shadows. "Jacob? Daniel?" she called. From the corner of her eye, she caught a flash of white. She turned her head, but nothing was there. She turned back to the spot where she'd been looking before and saw white again . . . this time she knew what it was . . . the swishing tail of a cat. And behind the cat, the happy tramp of men's feet.

She was rescued!

"I'm over here!" she called, waving her arms wildly.

"Meriwether?" she heard a familiar voice. "What are you doing out here?" Daniel rushed to her side and frowned down at her, hands on hips. His reddish hair was wet and swiped to one side, and beneath his vest a thin, white shirt clung to his chest. Meriwether thought she had never seen a more friendly sight in her life.

Jacob bent to inspect her ankle, "Twisted, I'd say." Daniel looked back in confusion, but quickly put two and two together.

"I wanted to get a better look at the lake," explained Meriwether feebly. "I stepped back and tripped . . . must've hit my head," her hand felt unconsciously at the cut. "I tried, but I can't walk. Would've hopped, but I was afraid I'd slip and really get myself in a mess!"

Daniel rolled his eyes and squatted down beside Meriwether. "Way to go, Grace," he grinned.

Jacob removed her shoe and grunted, "Next time ye go traipsin' through the forest, ye might want t' reconsider yer footwear."

Meriwether nodded. She deserved a telling off. "You're right, Jacob. I'm sorry. What will Mrs. Meriwether say?"

Jacob grunted again and rubbed at the stubble on his chin, "Nothin' good, I 'spect.

"Well, best get ye back and face the music."

He bent down and picked Meriwether up easily. Meriwether knew he wasn't really angry with her, just worried. She put her arms about his neck to help support herself and inhaled the pungent, earthy smells of tobacco, sweat, and dirt.

Her head still felt oddly light. She could feel herself drifting, but there was one thing she needed to know, "How, how did you find me?"

"Aye," answered Jacob in a grumbly whisper, "ye've got Artemis t' thank fer that."

Meriwether revived a bit as they reached the manor house. Jacob rang the bell and Mary, who answered the door, immediately began fussing over Meriwether. "Tell 'em I'm takin' the miss upstairs to 'er room," Jacob told Mary. "I'll be down t' explain in a bit."

Meriwether wasn't sure he'd be able to make it up the stairs . . . it was a long, steep climb . . . but he managed. Daniel followed skulkingly behind, trying to blend into the woodwork. By the time he had her up the stairs, Mary was already there running Meriwether a scalding hot bath. Meriwether had no idea how she had delivered the message to the Meriwethers and beaten them there, unless there were stairs Meriwether was not yet aware of . . . but she wondered on this only vaguely as Jacob and Daniel left her in Mary's proficient hands.

Mary peeled the wet and muddy clothing off of Meriwether, who was so anxious to get into the bath that she forgot to be embarrassed, then helped her climb into the deep tub without hurting her ankle.

It was heaven. Absolute heaven.

Meriwether closed her eyes and mind, allowing herself to feel only the warmth of the water against her skin, the silken weight of it as Mary poured it from a pitcher and gently washed her hair. She must have fallen asleep in the bath because Mary tapped her on the shoulder and she woke up.

" Meriwether, the doctor's here to look at tha' ankle. Here, let me help ye out o' there . . . tha's a girl," she said, heaving Meriwether out and wrapping her in a towel in one deft move. Mary dried her off like a baby, then slipped one of Meriwether's own nightgowns over her head. She helped Meriwether into her room and onto her bed and brushed her hair while the doctor, a young man with serious, dark eyes and unruly dark hair gently felt her ankle.

His fingers were long and sinewy -- like her father's, but more delicate. Meriwether watched as he turned and prodded her ankle, then held her breath as his handsome face studied the nasty gash above her right temple. The doc was a dreamboat, to borrow an expression of Holly's. At last he spoke in a slow, thoughtful voice, "Your ankle is not broken, . . . Miss Knight, I believe?" Meriwether nodded. "However, it is badly sprained and needs wrapping . . . and rest. No more exploring for you . . . at least for a few days."

"Yes sir," answered Meriwether. Her voice sounded croaky from lack of use. He reached up to brush the hair back from her face and frowned, "What I'm worried about is this cut. Have you been in and out of consciousness?"

Meriwether hedged, "Well . . . ."

"Yes sir, she has," piped Mary. "Fell asleep in the bath just now, she did."

"Um-hmm," replied the good doctor, top lip between thumb and forefinger. "Mary, is it? . . ."

Mary nodded and flushed violently.

"Mary, you must keep a very careful eye on our

patient. I'll need to speak with you privately in a moment." Again, Mary nodded vigorously . . . the flush deepening and spreading down her neck into her collar. He took some gauze from his doctor's bag and wrapped Meriwether's foot as he spoke, "I'll be back to see you in the morning. Rest well, small one." He took her face in his hand and smiled, the first one Meriwether had seen. "Mary?" he said as he walked from the room.

Mary hopped obediently from the bed and followed the doctor out into the hall. They shut the door all but a crack. Meriwether could see him talking and Mary nodding, but she couldn't hear what they were saying. She tried, but the strain of it made her head ache.

Presently, Mary came back into the room. "Dr. Willowsby says t' take two a these, an' for me t' watch ye as ye sleep. Now he's down t' look on your grandfather," she said, handing Meriwether two small pills and a glass of water.

"Gulp," Meriwether swallowed the medicine, "what's wrong with Col. Meriwether?"

"Yer gettin' hurt upset him somethin' terrible. Mrs. Meriwether's been seein' to 'im . . . that's why she ain't up here with ye. She dotes on 'im, she does," Mary explained as she plumped Meriwether's pillows and helped her to lay back into a comfortable position.

Meriwether frowned and Mary rushed on, "Not that it's yer fault. No one blames ye fer whot happened! Yer lucky it was nothin' worse!"

Meriwether awarded Mary the slightest of grins to lighten the mood, but she doubted Mrs. Meriwether felt the same way. She had upset her grandfather . . . made him worse. Meriwether felt just awful.

Mary brought in an armchair from another room and settled herself into it with some embroidery. Meriwether watched her fingers as they deftly wielded the needle and thread . . . in and out . . . in and out.

The pills did their work, and as the pain subsided from her ankle and her head ceased to throb, Meriwether fell asleep.

Chapter Ten

Next morning, Meriwether awoke to a tray full of good things to eat, compliments of Martha Cook. Mary had dark circles underneath her eyes, and Meriwether hoped she hadn't stayed in the chair all night watching her sleep -- but she probably had.

As she ate, Dr. Willowsby knocked lightly on her door and stuck his head in. "How's our patient?" he asked seriously, his long, black trousered legs carrying him to her bedside.

Meriwether smiled, "I'm good . . . head hurts a little."

"I've brought you a prescription for that . . . and crutches for you to use until the ankle mends." Dr. Willowsby fetched the crutches and demonstrated how to use them properly -- so as not to irritate the sensitive skin underneath her arms. "Now you try."

Meriwether hung her legs over the side of her bed and put her weight on her good ankle. Even beneath the wrapping, she could tell that the right one was severely swollen. Dr. Willowsby adjusted the height of the crutch, then let her have a go. It wasn't easy, but Meriwether eventually made it all the way across the room and back to her bed . . . . She was exhausted!

Well, at least I can take myself to the bathroom, she thought, grateful for small favors.

"Now I want you to get plenty of rest, and that means both of you," he said, eyeing the girls. "You've had a long night of it, Mary," she blushed uncontrollably whenever he said her name, "so I expect you to take it easy today."

Mary stifled a yawn, "Thank ye, Dr. Willowsby, but I must be tendin' to me chores. T'day's washin' day, ye see, and I'll be right busy."

Dr. Willowsby's handsome face frowned, "But you stayed up all night. I'll speak to Lillian. . . surely she would let you have the day off."

"No!" cried Mary, rushing to the doctor. "Please doan't say nothin' to Mrs. Meriwether. I'm all righ', really I am!"

Dr. Willowsby studied her quizzically. "Very well, then," he said at last. He turned back to Meriwether, "You're young, and I expect you'll heal quickly. Use the crutches until it doesn't hurt to put any weight on the ankle . . . and . . . and stay out of the trees."

Meriwether nodded, *that was an odd thing to say*, and Dr. Willowsby let himself out the door, "Ladies."

As soon as he was gone, Mary fell backwards on the bed in an exaggerated swoon. Meriwether smiled, "Pretty cute, huh?"

Mary put her hands to her cheeks and turned her head to face Meriwether, "*Cute* doesn't even begin to cover it! I swear, I can 'ardly remember me own name when 'e looks at me!"

"He's awfully young to be a doctor," said Meriwether.

"Aye, he's workin' beside 'is father, learnin' the patients, gatherin' people's trust before old Doc Willowsby either retires or dies . . . whichever comes first," replied Mary.

"Oh."

Mary sat up and looked furtively over her shoulder to make sure no one was listening, "His mum's gone round the pike, poor thing."

Meriwether didn't get it, "Round the pike?"

"She's crazy as a loon . . . completely insane . . . lost 'er mind years ago, but old Dr. Willowsby won't put 'er away. They keep 'er locked up in that big 'ouse in town. Young Dr. Willowsby will never marry . . . not with 'is mum alive, and it's a shame, a right shame . . . all that loveliness gone t' waste."

"Oh," said Meriwether again. It was all she could think to say.

Mary leaned forward and put her hand on top of Meriwether's, "Anyways, I shouldna' said nothin', bein' as how Mrs. Willowsby is yer grandmother's sister and all." The pleading look on Mary's face was almost tearful.

Meriwether was taken aback, "What? You mean that Dr. Willowsby . . .," Meriwether pictured the family tree in her head, "Dr. Willowsby is my cousin?"

"Well, 'e's yer mother's cousin, so technically that makes 'im yer second cousin," rattled Mary. She yawned again, "I best be gettin' to the washin'. It won't do itself!" and she left.

Meriwether felt like a land mine had gone off in her room. Up until now, she could have counted on two hands the number of relatives she knew herself to have. Grandmother, Granddaddy, Aunt Phil, Uncle Roger, cousins Claire and Collin, her father, her mother, Col. and Mrs. Meriwether. Two of the ten were dead, and one other was close to it. But here was an entirely new, unexpected branch of relations. Mrs. Willowsby, her mother's aunt, insane. Her husband. Her son.

Had Meriwether's mother and young Dr. Willowsby played together when they were children? And what might he be able to tell her of her mother, of their secrets, her dreams?

Meriwether lay back on her pillow and looked out into the back garden. She imagined them playing there, the fair haired girl and the dark little boy, splashing each other in the pool and hiding in trees to avoid coming in for tea. The image was so powerful that Meriwether had to close her eyes and give her head a firm shake.

Stay out of the trees.

There were ghosts in this house, she decided. Ghosts and secrets.

Chapter Eleven

Back at work in the orchard, Daniel thought back to last night and how they had found Meriwether. She said she had tripped and fallen. The rock she had hit her head on was easy enough to see, but in the darkness, Daniel had been unable to find what she had stumbled on in the first place. He planned on going back to the spot after Greene let him off and doing some more searching.

It troubled him, and he wasn't sure why. It was a very Meriwether like thing to do . . . traipsing off into the forest without proper clothing, oblivious to the possible dangers. Still, he had sensed something in the wood, and although he'd never admit it to a living soul, he'd been glad of Greene's company.

Artemis, of course, was a mystery. *Was that normal cat behavior?* Daniel shrugged as he lifted the long pole with the blade attached and began to saw back and forth on the errant branch. Somewhere he'd heard that truth was stranger than fiction, and he guessed it must be so.

He was glad he'd come. It was obvious that Meriwether needed protecting. From what, was the question.

As he worked, biceps quivering with effort, something niggled at the back of his brain. A flash of white disappearing into the darkness . . . into the trees.

Chapter Twelve

  Because of her ankle, and despite the crutches, Meriwether was basically confined to her room for at least the day. She worked on homework for a bit, wondering vaguely whether or not she was to have a tutor. English, science, and history were no problem, but algebra was proving a bit difficult. Meriwether knew it was bad when re-reading the directions left her more confused than she had been in the first place.
  Frustrated, Meriwether leaned back on her pillow, closed her eyes, and fell asleep. She woke up an hour or so later to a heavy thump at the bottom of her bed. The white cat was purring and cleaning himself against her good leg.
  "How did you get in here?" Meriwether asked him.
  He looked at her through emerald orbs and resumed his toilette. Meriwether sat up, and as she did so, noticed that someone had come in while she was napping and cranked open the window. Probably Mary. Outside the window were the branches of a large linden tree.
  "Climbed the tree, did you?" said Meriwether, resisting the urge to scratch the cat behind his ears. If she did, she would need to go wash her hands, or else risk setting off her allergies, and the trek to the bathroom was simply not worth it. "Now what did Jacob say your name

was?" she mused, trying to remember. "Abercrombie? . . . No, it was something Greek . . . or maybe Roman . . . Aphrodite? . . . No, that's closer though . . . it was definitely an 'A' name . . . something Ar--, Art--, Artemis! That's it, Artemis!"

Meriwether was very pleased with herself; the cat just looked at her as if she wasn't quite right in the head. Actually, she *wasn't* feeling quite right. Stitches hadn't been necessary since the cut, really not very deep, was located inside the hair line, but the pain of it was starting to come back in a dull and droning thud.

Her medicine was on the table beside her, but she wasn't sure how long she was supposed to wait between doses. Her watch told her it was nearly lunch time, so she decided to tough it out and wait for her tray. Then she could ask if it would be all right to take another pill.

She lay back again on her pillow and closed her eyes against the mounting pain. Artemis abandoned his nest beside her leg and curled up on her chest. Meriwether pushed him off, but, not to be daunted, he came right back and settled heavily in the same spot. His white fur tickled Meriwether's nose. She sneezed, and with an ugly look, Artemis pranced to the bottom of the bed.

"I tried to tell you," said Meriwether, sniffling. "Achoo!"

Great, she thought. *Now I need to wash my face.* She swung her legs over the side of the bed and situated her crutches. Before standing, she gave Artemis a quick scratch on the top of his head and underneath his chin. She was going to the bathroom anyway . . . why not?

Meriwether hobbled to the bathroom, and while she was in there, decided to take full advantage of the situation. Her head was really pounding by now and she wished she had brought the medicine bottle into the bathroom with her. She was already tired from the short trek, and the thought of going all the way back into the bedroom, retrieving the bottle, and then back to the bathroom for some water was more than she could bear. So to save time and energy, Meriwether filled a glass from the sink with water and clumsily attempted to carry it back with her to the bed, water sloshing on the stone floor as she tried to maneuver the crutches and hold on to the glass at the same time.

The glass began to slip in her hand. She was nearly there, though. *I can make it . . . I can make it*, she willed her fingers to hold on to the slippery glass. Almost there . . . one more step . . . Crash! The glass slipped from her fingers at the very last moment, splintering into a thousand shards against the floor.

At that same moment, Mrs. Meriwether opened the door to her room bearing a tray of lunch. Her mouth flattened into a tight line as she took the bell from her pocket and gave it a jangle. "Tell me Meriwether," she said as she set down the tray and went to help Meriwether back into bed, her shoes crunching on the shattered glass, "are you always this much trouble?"

"I'm sorry . . . I . . . my head hurt," Meriwether ended lamely, sinking against the pillows.

"And what are you doing in here?" Mrs. Meriwether eyed Artemis reproachfully. Artemis took his time, stretched, then padded to the window, leaping lightly to the sill and onto an outstretched tree branch. To Meriwether she said, "I do not allow cats in the house. I'm allergic."

Meriwether determined, then and there, not to be allergic to cats anymore.

"Yes ma'am," Meriwether replied, not wanting to get Mary in trouble for opening the window. Her eyes were starting to water now from the pain in her head, and the smell of food was turning her stomach. She looked longingly at the pills beside her, and Mrs. Meriwether seemed to notice. Crunching back over to the food tray, she brought back a cup of tea and measured out two pills into Meriwether's hand. Meriwether swallowed the medicine gratefully, and closing her eyes, waited for the throbbing to abate.

She heard Mary come in and clean up the mess. No one said a word. Mary left, and still Mrs. Meriwether sat.

Slowly, the meds began to kick in. The food that nauseated her a moment ago now smelled delicious. "I'm better now," she said to Mrs. Meriwether. "Is that beef stew?" Meriwether sniffed the air.

Mrs. Meriwether took the hint and brought Meriwether the tray. "It may have gotten cold, but Martha does make an excellent Irish stew. Col. Meriwether requested it today. He likes the broth. I offered to bring it up because I want to talk to you."

Meriwether sipped at her soup as Mrs. Meriwether talked. It was still warm, which meant it must have been steaming hot when Mrs. Meriwether first brought it in.

"I feel that your accident was partly my fault because I gave you free reign of the grounds. I never dreamed you would venture so far, which was silly of me because you are, obviously, your mother's child. There are -- dangers -- in the forest . . . in any wild place," Mrs. Meriwether looked at her hands, at the bed frame, out the window, anywhere but straight at Meriwether. She seemed very uncomfortable and worried a tissue in her hands to shreds. "I've noticed that Mr. Greene has a young charge working with him. He'll be a local boy who is well versed in our . . . terrain. Once your ankle is healed, if you must do more exploring, I will expect you to take the boy with you. I'll let Mr. Greene know what I expect . . . that he is to let the boy go with you whenever you like."

This was too good to be true! Meriwether's spirits lifted immediately, but she dared not show it. "Yes ma'am," she said. "Thank you."

"Very good. Now you've finished your soup, I must see to Col. Meriwether. His heart is so frail, and I'm afraid you gave him quite a shock coming in like that. Clearly, we must postpone your meeting," Mrs. Meriwether went on.

Meriwether winced under the thick layer of guilt, but she did have a question and she intended to ask it. "Mrs. Meriwether?" she didn't know what else to call the woman, "Am I to have a tutor? Your letter said I would, but the thing is, I don't . . . ."

"I've been unable to locate anyone willing to come," which was an odd way of putting it. "With what subjects do you need assistance?" Mrs. Meriwether now appeared back in control and pierced Meriwether with a beady gaze.

"Just math, really," swallowed Meriwether, feeling like the biggest dunce ever. "Everything else is fine."

Mrs. Meriwether nodded curtly, "Not a problem. I taught mathematics for a short time. I'm sure I can help you through it."

"Oh, all right," Meriwether wasn't sure whether to be relieved or depressed. "It's algebra. Do you know algebra?"

Again the penetrating stare, "I think I can manage."

All in all, it hadn't been a bad interview, Meriwether thought as she stared out the window, her tummy nice and full from the fortifying stew. No tutor, Daniel's company whenever she wanted it, and a large slice of guilt on the side. Well, two out of three wasn't bad.

Meriwether could not, in all honesty, say that she liked her grandmother. Mrs. Meriwether was prickly and distant, and of course there was the issue of Meriwether's mother. Despite what she had seen of the old woman, however, Meriwether was confused. Lillian Meriwether was cold . . . but did not seem totally heartless. Could she really have abandoned her own daughter when she needed her most?

Beneath her window, Daniel and Mr. Greene were carting and shoveling out mounds of fertilizer into the plant beds. Daniel was whistling, and a few strains of his airy melody made their way up to Meriwether so that she knew he was there even though she couldn't see him. Artemis appeared again in the window, leaping gracefully from the tree branch he used as a bridge between his two worlds.

"You're not supposed to be in here," Meriwether wagged her finger at him.

Artemis purred and commenced to licking himself at the foot of her bed, and Meriwether smiled, happy to rebel in some small way.

Chapter Thirteen

The next few days passed. They did not pass quickly, but they did pass.

Each day, Meriwether got her exercise by using her crutches up and down the long hallway outside of her room. Her meals were brought to her, and she got a lot of school work done. Mrs. Meriwether came every evening before dinner and went over the math she'd tackled that day. It was starting to make more, if not perfect, sense, and Meriwether's only worry was that she was learning to do the problems Mrs. Meriwether's way . . . not her teacher's. Mrs. Meriwether refused to even look at the book, insisting her method was best.

By the time she was able to put some pressure on her ankle, she was at least a week ahead in her studies and anxiously looking forward to rambling about with Daniel . . . she intended to obey Mrs. Meriwether completely on that point.

She had managed to get some information about her grandfather out of Mary and knew that he was not well, he would never be well again, but that he had at least recovered from the shock of her injury and was stable -- but resting. Mrs. Meriwether had not mentioned meeting him again, and because Meriwether knew that she was there at his request, wondered that something had not been arranged. Especially now that her ankle was feeling better, she felt sure she could make it down the stairs if they'd let her.

If they'd let her?

The thought shocked her. What had she become . . . a docile prisoner? They might baby her forever if she didn't prove she was better!

Careful of her ankle, she hurried as fast as she could to get dressed before anyone else came in her room and tried to stop her. She unwrapped the ankle and tried it out . . . felt pretty good . . . and the swelling had gone down sufficiently to wear the socks and Converse sneakers she laced on her feet. They were high tops and, Meriwether thought, gave her just the right amount of support.

Meriwether walked to her door and listened. She couldn't hear anything, so she cracked the door an inch and peeked out into the hall. Empty . . . *good.*

Trying hard to be quiet, she made her way down the stairs, from the bottom of which she could see Mrs. Meriwether at her writing desk in the blue room. Her back was to Meriwether. The taste of freedom was sweet on her lips, and she felt a longing ache to be outside. She was afraid that if Mrs. Meriwether saw her, she would stop her, so she crept along the entry hall, intent on not making a single sound. She held her breath as she opened the heavy front door.

Creak!

Meriwether froze, her heart hammering in her chest, straining for the efficient click clack of her grandmother's low heels.

Nothing happened.

Creak . . . creak . . . she was out!

Heady with her success, she skipped down the stone steps and fairly jogged around the side of the house opposite from Mrs. Meriwether and closer to the gardener's cottage. Impressed, she balanced against a tree and circled her ankle round and about. She was completely healed!

She heard voices. Daniel and Mr. Greene must not be far. Through a grove of pines, Meriwether followed a footpath toward the sound and emerged into a small clearing where she found the gardener and his hand cutting and stacking firewood into a growing pile.

"Meriwether!" shouted Daniel, sinking his axe into an upright timber, and splitting it with a satisfying thwack!

Jacob removed his cap and held it to his chest, "Good to see ye out an' about."

"Thanks!" said Meriwether. "But please don't tell Mrs. Meriwether. I, uh, sort of snuck out," Jacob frowned at her from beneath scraggly brows, "but my ankle feels fine," she demonstrated by circling and wagging her ankle back and forth. "See?"

"I did na' hear nothin' . . . I did na' see nothin'," Jacob said seriously.

Meriwether beamed, "Thanks, Jacob!"

"I suppose ye're wantin' t' steal me help, then," the corners of his mouth twitched, and Meriwether knew he didn't mind.

"Just for a little while. Come on, Daniel!" she beckoned.

Daniel walked along beside Meriwether with his hands in his pockets, whistling a tune, happy to have a break from work. Mr. Greene never stopped, not as long as the sun was up, anyhow, and even though Daniel was getting used to the schedule, he was beginning to think he'd gotten himself into a bit more than he'd bargained for.

"How's work?" asked Meriwether, grinning uncontrollably with her newfound liberty.

Daniel shrugged. "S'okay. How's *the manor*?" he said with a nasty inflection.

Meriwether scowled, not sure how to take him. "It's fine," she said testily. She stopped smiling and faced forward, the wind in her face as they continued to walk, unconsciously, back toward the cliff's edge where she had fallen. Why was he ruining this?

Realizing he had offended her, Daniel nudged her with his elbow, "Sorry, eh? Guess I'm just jealous is all."

"Jealous?" retorted Meriwether, incredulous. "Jealous that I've been holed up in my room for days doing homework -- being tutored by my grandmother? Jealous that I've had a running headache for the last four or five days? Jealous that . . . ."

"Okay, okay," laughed Daniel, sounding like his old self, "I give! Said I was sorry, didn't I? No need to go all postal on me!"

Meriwether was still mad, but blowing her stack had made her feel a little better, "Yeah, well . . . you asked for it."

They walked in silence for a bit. Somewhere above them, a bird released its haunting cry. Meriwether shivered. Was it getting colder? "So, your *grandmother* is your tutor?" asked Daniel.

"Well, just for math."

"Maths," corrected Daniel.

"Math," she said again, forcefully.

Neither one of them looked at each other, but they both knew the other was smiling. The ice broken, they began to talk companionably. Meriwether told Daniel about her visit from young Dr. Willowsby and what Mary had told her about his mother, and Daniel told Meriwether about how Artemis had yowled at them until they'd followed him to find her in the woods.

"He's some cat," said Meriwether, and as she spoke, he appeared there, suddenly beside them, swishing his tail and looking up at them with his large green eyes.

"Meow."

"Some cat," agreed Daniel as they reached the tree line and stood on the precipice overlooking Blelham Tarn.

"She thinks you're a local boy," said Meriwether. "That's why she wants you with me when I poke around. My mother must have done the same thing . . . she said something about it."

Daniel nodded with new understanding, "I wondered what the deal was. She must have said something to Mr. Greene, but he never told me anything. I couldn't believe it when he let me off. He loves to work, that man! Eat, sleep, work -- that's all he does . . . all he wants to do!"

"Yes, she said she would speak to him about it." Then switching topics, "I guess that's how he's made it around here so long. Leaves Mrs. Meriwether without anything to complain about."

"Still calling her 'Mrs. Meriwether', I see," said Daniel. "What about your grandfather -- have you met him?"

"Not yet. I think it threw him for a loop when you brought me in like that. He's been in bed for days, and don't think I haven't heard about it!" Meriwether's voice softened, "I want to meet him though. If my getting hurt affected him so much, he must be different . . . different from Mrs. Meriwether anyway."

They stood in silence for a few moments, taking in the dramatic panorama splayed before them. It looked like a picture postcard, the reds and yellows of an English autumn interspersed among the evergreens that lined the lake, and Meriwether breathed deeply of the cool, crisp air. A gust of wind blew suddenly from behind, whipping her hair into her eyes and mouth. She reached inside her jacket pocket for a hair tie and pulled her wind-blown tresses into a messy pony-tail. Her ears were cold, but at least her hair was out of her face.

Daniel pulled his cap down lower over his forehead and turned the collar of his jacket up. "I've been up here a time or two, looking for what made you trip that night," said Daniel, not looking at Meriwether. "Didn't find nothin'."

Meriwether turned and swept the ground with the toe of her shoe, Artemis at her feet. Artemis leapt onto the jutting rock Meriwether had fallen against, curling his tail around him, "Meow."

Meriwether crouched beside the cat, "What is it, Artemis? Are you trying to tell us something?"

"Meow." Artemis slunk down off the rock, looked at Meriwether, then looked back at the rock, "Meow."

Meriwether peered more closely at the rock, rubbing away some of the moss that covered its face. She gasped, "Oh, my gosh! Daniel, come look at this!"

"What is it?" he said, stooping down beside her.

"I've found something . . . I think it's writing. Help me clear this moss," Meriwether said excitedly.

They made quick work of it, and Meriwether squinted at the etchings that now clearly stood out against the gray bit of granite. "ATHENA," read Meriwether, and then in smaller letters, "F.M., J.W, J.G." Meriwether's stomach did a lurching sort of flip. This was a grave.

She jumped back automatically, and Daniel looked up at her strangely, "What's wrong?"

"Someone's buried here," Meriwether said, her voice quavering slightly.

Daniel's eyes went from her to the stone, then back to her, "Nah."

"What do you mean, 'nah'?" cried Meriwether, trying for control. "It's obvious that's a headstone! Someone named Athena is buried here, and you're kneeling right on top of the grave!"

Daniel actually smiled. Meriwether could not believe it!

"Haven't you ever had a pet, Meriwether?" he asked the ghost of a chuckle behind the words.

"What? . . . . Of course I . . . well, no, actually . . . have you?" that was a stupid thing to say.

"Well, yeah, I have," answered Daniel, positively beaming. "His name was Sparky, and he's buried in my backyard at home."

"Oh," said Meriwether. "I'm sorry, but *why* are you smiling?"

"Because this Athena is not a some*one*, she's a some*thing* . . . a pet?" he explained as if Meriwether were a toddler, incapable of normal, rational routes of reasoning.

"Oh," she said again, feeling very dense indeed.

"Meow," said Artemis in confirmation.

"Who was Athena?" Meriwether asked Artemis.

"Did you know her?"

Artemis gazed widely at Meriwether, then jumped back on the rock, curled into a ball, and began licking himself. The language divide was too great.

Meriwether knelt again and reread the initials, "**F.M.**, that's my mother, Felicia Meriwether. **J.W.** . . W . . . Willowsby! Dr. Willowsby . . . first name J...and **J.G.** . . .," *could it possibly be*? "Do you think . . .?"

"Cool," breathed Daniel as he looked over Meriwether's shoulder. His warm breath touched the curls at the back of her neck and she shivered. Flushing, she stood up abruptly, one shoulder, in her haste, catching Daniel squarely under the chin as she rose.

"Ouch!" he yelped.

Meriwether winced, feeling his pain, "Sorry!" *I'm such a dork!* she thought, cursing herself. She went to the edge of the cliff and stood with her back turned to Daniel, trying to regain her composure. A sudden thought crept into her mind and she turned back toward him, her embarrassment forgotten. Daniel was still scowling and rubbing his chin.

"You know what this means, don't you?" said Meriwether. "My mom used to come here . . . to this spot. I mean, this is where she chose to bury her pet . . . so it must have been special to her." Meriwether paced up and down, her mouth speaking the thoughts her brain was forming as fast as she could get them out, "And don't you think it's odd that this is the place I came to -- my very first day here -- not even knowing where I was going? And then Artemis found me . . . and he obviously wanted us to see the gravestone . . . something strange is going on here, Daniel! I can feel it!" she ended dramatically.

Daniel looked at her skeptically, "I don't know, Meriwether. I think maybe you're reading too much into it. I mean, yeah, he's a smart cat . . . but he's just a cat."

Meriwether stood there a moment staring at Daniel, her eyes blazing. There were a thousand things she wanted to say, but she didn't say any of them, and then just as quickly as the revelation came, it disappeared. She was no longer certain of anything and suddenly felt dull and deflated. "I think we should head back," she said in a low voice, "my ankle is starting to hurt."

Chapter Fourteen

The walk back up to the house took a long time. Meriwether's ankle truly was beginning to ache. Daniel patiently took her arm and helped her over the roots and rocks that obstructed their path. Meriwether appreciated it, but she was a million miles away.

Was someone, somewhere trying to communicate something? Meriwether had never believed in spirits, not really, but she felt the whisper of long ago things stirring the very air she was breathing. And she couldn't talk to anyone about it . . . that's what made it so awful. Maybe Holly would have understood, but Daniel was a boy.

To Meriwether, that explained everything.

Meriwether Manor loomed in front of them as they emerged from the trees and into the waning light of late afternoon. Meriwether caught her reflection in the pool as they passed, her white face and dark eyes staring dolefully out of the water and back at her.

"Thanks, Daniel; I'd better take it from here."

"Will you be in trouble?" he asked, eyes anxious underneath the bill of his cap.

Meriwether shrugged, "Dunno."

"You okay, Meriwether?"

Meriwether shoved her hands in her pockets and

nodded, stamping her feet against the cold that had crept up on them as the sun went down. "Um, hmm."

Not convinced, Daniel shrugged, "I reckon I've got no idea what I'm talking about anyway. Maybe he is some sort of magic cat or something."

Meriwether smiled, *magic cat*, really! She rolled her eyes and waved as she turned her back to Daniel. Surely her absence had been noticed by now. She was not naive enough to imagine that she could make it back in and up the stairs without anyone being the wiser. Taking a deep breath, she marched right up to the first door she saw with lights coming out of its windows and let herself in, steeling for whatever punishment lay in store.

"Well, an' there she is . . . the naughty wee lassie! Disappearin' an' leavin' us all to worry 'bout ye, like," Martha Cook bustled over, wiping floury hands on an ample, aproned front.

"I'm sorry," said Meriwether. "Is she very mad?"

"Towerin', I suspect," winked Martha, patting her on the back and leading her to a rocking chair beside a crackling kitchen fire. "Ye look plumb froze to death! Bes' let me get ye a cup o' tea an' a biscuit. How about some soup . . . would ye like some soup?"

Meriwether smiled, "Soup would be great, thanks." *The last meal of a condemned man? Well then, so be it.*

The fire felt wonderful, and after a few minutes of happily sipping her tea, she took off the jacket and propped her feet on an embroidered stool that was pushed against the hearth. Martha brought her a tea table and Meriwether slurped the soup hungrily.

Martha left the kitchen, Meriwether supposed to inform her grandmother that she had returned. *I should probably be nervous*, she thought lazily as she closed her eyes and rested her head against the rocker. The soup settled warmly in her stomach. Meriwether could feel herself drifting.

She was walking along the forest path beside her mother. Felicia was young, and just Meriwether's size, with long ash blonde curls streaming down her back. They held hands and giggled conspiratorially as they emerged onto the clearing.
　"*Go on . . . look!*" *said the girl, urging Meriwether to stand right at the edge and look over.*
　Meriwether did. The lake and trees seemed a million miles away. Vertigo rushed in Meriwether's ears as her mother smiled and nodded at her side.
　Then from behind she felt a sharp push. Someone screamed. Losing her balance, Meriwether began to fall.

　Meriwether jolted awake in her chair; her heart was beating wildly in her chest and her hand flew shakily to the locket at her throat. What was *that*? And from somewhere, way in the back of her mind, floated the answer . . . *a warning*.
　Meriwether didn't want to believe it.
　It seemed far too incredible.
　Could it be? Could it be that she was in danger here?
　Stay out of the trees . . . . Dr. Willowsby knew something! She was sure of it! Daniel could be a skeptic all he wanted, but Meriwether knew -- suddenly and terribly -- that she'd better start paying attention . . . she'd better be careful.

Mrs. Cook bustled back into the kitchen and cleared Meriwether's empty soup bowl from the folding tray at her lap. "Would ye like some pudding, dearie?" she asked kindly.

Meriwether, not one to turn down dessert on even the direst of occasions, nodded, "Oh yes, thank you . . . . Did you -- er -- did you talk to Mrs. Meriwether?"

"I did." Mrs. Cook cut a large wedge of pie and topped it off with a dollop of fresh whipped cream.

Meriwether waited . . . , "And?"

Waddling over, she set the pie down in front of Meriwether, "An' there's no use tryin' t' fool Mrs. Meriwether, I can tell ye that much. Heard ye sneakin' down the stairs, she did, and checked with Mr. Greene t' make sure ye took the boy."

"Oh," said Meriwether. So much for her stealth skills.

"Col. Meriwether's doin' a might better, an' she says fer you t' plan t' meet 'im in the mornin'. Breakfast in the dinin' room, 8:00 sharp, an' do na' be late!"

Meriwether repeated the instructions to herself, determined not to oversleep and mess it all up.

"Doan't ye worry, dearie. Mary'll be there at 7:00 to wake ye up an' help ye get dressed. It's important fer ye t' make a good impression with the colonel. He doted on yer mother so . . . wouldna' want to disappoint 'im!"

Great, thought Meriwether, *nothing like a bit of pressure.*

"Ye like the pie, then," said Mrs. Cook, beaming at Meriwether's empty plate.

"Wha . . . oh, yes, very much. Thank you," she realized she'd eaten the whole thing without tasting it.

What a waste!

Chapter Fifteen

The next morning, Mary nudged her gently awake. Pale, early light mottled through the thick glass of the windows. Artemis lay at the foot of her bed, and Meriwether had no idea how he'd gotten there.

Mary opened the window and picked up the cat, "Shoo!" she said, practically pitching him out onto the branch. "Ye're not supposed t' be in here!"

Meriwether tested her ankle out beneath the covers. She was afraid she'd overdone it yesterday, but was pleased to find that everything felt fine.

"Go wash up an' I'll set yer clothes out for ye," Mary told her as she set to straightening the bed linens.

Quite sure she could manage choosing an outfit on her own, Meriwether obeyed with sleepy abandon. Probably, Mrs. Meriwether had chosen what she wanted Meriwether to wear, and Mary was only doing her job . . . one she apparently needed, desperately.

When she got back from the bathroom, face washed, teeth and hair brushed and shining, she saw her most conservative ensemble laid out on the bed. Meriwether shrugged . . . *whatever*.

She dressed quickly. The room was cold, and it seemed like a naked eternity between the moment she shucked her pajama bottoms and was able to wiggle into the cream cabled tights. The soft, pleated drop waist skirt and red cashmere sweater felt like heaven. Grandmother had loved this outfit, declaring it a perfectly classic pairing that would never go out of style. Apparently, Mrs. Meriwether felt the same way.

Meriwether looked at herself in the mirror. This was what happened when a person let their grandmothers dress them.

"Good," said Mary as she walked around Meriwether, making sure everything was all right. "Now go!" Meriwether got the feeling that if she had been as light as the cat, Mary would have picked her up and thrown her out the door as unceremoniously as she had Artemis.

Breakfast this morning was being served in the formal dining room, a room that Meriwether had not yet visited due to her injury and days of meals in bed. It was a long, narrow room domineered by a large rectangular table of rich, dark wood. Twelve chairs flanked the table, but places were set for only three.

Colonel and Mrs. Meriwether sat in full regalia, and Col. Meriwether made to stand as Meriwether entered the room, but Mrs. Meriwether held out a cautionary hand. He stopped mid-rise and took his seat.

"Meriwether, my dear," he said in a wavery sort of voice that, never-the-less, sounded much stronger than his body looked, "forgive the formality of our breakfast. I tend to be at my best early in the day, and this table is taller than the others . . . easier for me to maneuver my chair under."

His blue eyes twinkled merrily as he fingered his

full, white moustache. As she approached her grandfather, Meriwether realized it was not a normal dining room chair he sat in but a wheel chair pulled up to the table. A tartan blanket covered his legs.

Meriwether at once thought him charming and quite handsome. She stood beside him and he clasped her hand in both of his. He smelled faintly of pipe smoke.

"I'm so happy to meet you, my dear. Please, take a seat." He offered her the chair immediately to his left, his eyes crinkling as he smiled.

Meriwether sat and took a sip of her tea. She couldn't think what to say.

"You're ankle is better, I see," said Mrs. Meriwether, filling in the gap.

Meriwether nodded, "Yes, thank you . . . er, sorry about yesterday."

Col. Meriwether looked confused, "Yesterday?"

Was that a smile playing at Mrs. Meriwether's lips? It was gone so quickly, Meriwether could not be sure.

"Nothing to worry about, darling," said Mrs. Meriwether, patting his hand with a cosseting sort of simper.

Col. Meriwether accepted the vague assurance, "Not getting into any more scrapes, I hope?"

"No sir," Meriwether promised him.

"She's to take Mr. Greene's new boy with her from now on," Mrs. Meriwether said pointedly. "What's his name, Meriwether? David, Darrell . . . ?"

"Daniel," answered Meriwether.

"Daniel, yes."

"What is the lad's surname?" wondered Col. Meriwether. "I believe I know all the local families. I like to know who's working for me . . . especially if he's escorting my granddaughter about."

"I'll make a point to ask Mr. Greene," Mrs. Meriwether replied. "What do you think of him, Meriwether?"

Meriwether wanted to put in a good word for Daniel without sounding too eager. She somehow felt that either too strong a vote for or against might get him sacked. "He's fine," she shrugged, and Mrs. Meriwether nodded disively as Meriwether's neither here nor there answer hit its mark.

Mrs. Cook brought in a fruit tray and a basket of fresh-made breads. Meriwether spooned some melon balls and what looked like sliced banana nut loaf onto her plate. Mrs. Meriwether filled Col. Meriwether's cup with steaming, black coffee. As he lifted the cup to his lips, Col. Meriwether's eyes twinkled at Meriwether from above the delicate china rim. Meriwether wondered randomly if it was difficult for him to keep his moustaches clean.

They feasted on eggs Benedict topped with a particularly light and delicious hollandaise sauce. Meriwether tried to forget her nervousness and enjoy the meal, but every time she reached for her cut crystal juice glass, she hoped desperately that she would not spill the contents and make a fool of herself.

At last, breakfast was over, and Meriwether had somehow managed it. She took a great sigh of relief as Mrs. Cook removed their plates.

"Come, my dear. I wish to discuss something with you in my study," said Col. Meriwether, wheeling back and away from the table.

Meriwether walked beside her grandfather and

behind Mrs. Meriwether as she led the way to the colonel's study. It was a small, wood paneled room with a cheerful fire crackling in the grate, shelves and shelves of books, a desk, and several mismatched armchairs. The ugly, mounted head of a wildebeest stared at them morosely from its lookout above the mantel.

Meriwether perched on the end of one of the armchairs closest to the fire. Toes pointed against the floor she could hardly reach, she folded her hands on her knees and waited for Col. Meriwether to begin.

Col. Meriwether cleared his throat, "Meriwether, I wish you to know that I am a dying man." Meriwether's eyes grew round. She hadn't known what to expect . . . but it wasn't this! "I asked Lillian to arrange your coming because I very much wanted to meet you, and also because I felt it necessary to discuss with you certain details concerning the transfer of this estate into your property at the event of my death."

Col. Meriwether stopped, as if what he'd just said explained everything . . . as if what he'd said made any sense at all. "I'm sorry, sir," said Meriwether, "but I don't understand."

He cleared his throat again, a gravelly, phlegm-ridden cough, "When I die, Meriwether Manor, its grounds and acreage become yours, Meriwether. You are my sole heir."

Okay, that was clear enough. "Thank you, sir," gasped Meriwether, struggling for words, "but . . . but what about Mrs. Meriwether?" Meriwether chanced a look at her grandmother, but she was looking deeply into the fire, the look on her face inscrutable.

"For the time being, Lillian will, of course, remain

here and oversee the management of the estate, and any major decisions will be fielded by a board of trustees until you have come of age. I would ask that you allow your grandmother to live out the rest of her life here at the manor, if she so chooses."

Meriwether nodded, flustered, "Of course." She could not imagine turning Mrs. Meriwether out of her home, and it felt very strange to be asked permission.

"I would like to show you the farms and introduce you to our tenants, so that you are not a stranger to them, or them to you," continued Col. Meriwether.

Her attention drawn from the fire, Mrs. Meriwether looked concerned, "Do you think that wise, Lionel? What of your health? Surely Mr. Greene...."

"It is my responsibility," said Col. Meriwether gently. Mrs. Meriwether's eyebrow arched, and her lips cemented together into a firm line, but she said no more. "Tomorrow morning, then?" he said to Meriwether.

Meriwether nodded, "Yes, that's fine."

"Very good. Lillian?" Mrs. Meriwether stood and pushed her husband from the room as Meriwether looked slowly about her and tried to let it all sink in.

Hers.

All hers.

It was inconceivable, and it suddenly made her relationship with Mrs. Meriwether that much more tenuous. Still, she hadn't seemed surprised . . . not too happy, maybe . . . but definitely not surprised.

Is this the way things are done here in England?, wondered Meriwether. *Granddaddy didn't chuck Grandmother out of the house when he died* . . . okay, so she knew Col. Meriwether wasn't exactly *chucking* Mrs.

Meriwether out . . . and they had built the house together . . . it wasn't something that had been in his family for centuries . . . *but still* . . . .

Meriwether sat very still in her squashy chair, not quite sure what she was meant to do. Had she been dismissed? Would Mrs. Meriwether return after seeing Col. Meriwether to his room? Were they even going to his room? For all Meriwether knew, they were catching a noon flight to Paris . . . but she doubted it.

Shrugging to herself, she decided to go in search of Daniel. She needed to talk to someone, even though she planned to keep what her grandfather had told her to herself. It would sound too much like bragging to share the news with Daniel, and Meriwether thought with a cringe that this would eventually drive an even greater wedge between them. And what would Holly think? . . . . No, she could not tell her either -- not anytime soon.

Meriwether ran her fingers along the dark wood paneling as she searched for a door that would lead her outside. She was a bit turned around, never having been in this part of the house before, and found herself in a wide hall. The stone floor, beneath a thick layer of Oriental carpet, muffled her footsteps. From somewhere, a chill draft of wind whooshed through the hall and set the light fixture to swinging creakily, throwing weird shadows against the somber portraits that lined the walls.

Meriwether gulped and willed herself to keep walking, staunchly ignoring the hair that prickled at the back of her neck. Another invisible gust whipped through the room, billowing Meriwether's skirt and hair. CRASH!!! A large metal shield fell to the floor, reverberating like an eerie gong in waves down the hall.

Enough was enough; Meriwether ran for it.

The manor formed a labyrinth as Meriwether ran blindly from one room to another. She burst through door after door, finding neither human occupant nor a way outside . . . and still she ran, refusing to look behind her.

At last, she stumbled into a glass conservatory, and taking time only to note the excessively cold temperature of the room, which actually felt pretty good as she'd been running for some time, and the exceedingly large plants that towered above her in their enormous pots, Meriwether wrenched open the French doors and doubled over, panting against her knees, struggling for breath.

She felt very silly. What had she been afraid of after all? Very glad no one had witnessed her mad flight; Meriwether straightened her clothing, smoothed her hair, and giving herself a little full body shake, set out to look for Daniel.

It was another gray day. Mist rose up from the ground and visibility was low. Meriwether had to use her ears as much as her eyes to locate her friend and Mr. Greene, and eventually found them trimming shrubs along the front of the house.

Daniel took one look at her her and knew something was wrong, "What happened?"

Am I that transparent?, wondered Meriwether. "Nothing," she said. "Just needed some fresh air."

"Dressed like that?" Daniel eyed her strangely.

Meriwether looked down at herself, "Oh, yeah . . . I had breakfast with Col. and Mrs. Meriwether. I didn't choose the outfit," she added hastily, just to make things clear.

Artemis wove himself sinuously between her ankles,

purring loudly, and Mr. Greene tipped his cap between swipes with the secateurs.

"Hello, Jacob," she smiled.

"Doan't mind if ye take Daniel for a bit. He can help me finish up here while ye change, an' then I've got some piles t' burn in the back pasture," said Mr. Greene as he stood back from the hedge to check its shape.

Meriwether looked at Daniel, hanging back behind Mr. Greene's shoulder. He nodded vigorously. "Okay, thanks!" she said, turning toward the house. "Be back in a bit!"

Minutes later, she returned in jeans and a Texas Tech University sweatshirt Dr. Burrows had given her a few weeks ago during the dig out at her family's ranch. Her hair was pulled back in a pony-tail, and Daniel looked her up and down appreciatively, "That's better."

"I'm takin' some eggs t' the market in Hawkshead later this mornin' if the two of ye want t' come," suggested Mr. Greene. "Meriwether, I'll ask the missus for ye if ye be so inclined."

Meriwether nodded, "Oh, yes . . . that would be lovely!" She hadn't been to town yet, since the shopping trip to Thorpe's had been canceled, and was very curious to see it.

Jacob pulled at his cap and mashed the secateurs on top of the branches heaped high in his wheelbarrow. "Meet me here in an hour," he said as he pushed the wheelbarrow along the drive and toward his cottage.

Daniel took Meriwether's arm and whispered in her ear, "Quick, let's get out of here before he changes his mind!"

"How was your breakfast?" asked Daniel as they

walked. "You finally met your grandfather, I take it."

Meriwether nodded, "Yeah . . . er . . . it was good. We had eggs Benedict, and he was really nice. He's in a wheelchair." Meriwether watched her feet as she walked. She didn't want Daniel to see her face, and she wished they could change the subject. She hoped he hadn't noticed her odd, halting sentences.

"Why's he in a wheelchair?" Daniel wanted to know.

"Well, I suppose it's because his legs don't work," answered Meriwether cattily. "Maybe he was injured in the war . . . they do call him *Col.* Meriwether . . . or maybe he had a stroke. What kind of question is that . . . *Why's he in a wheelchair?*"

"Shows how much you know," said Daniel in a superior tone.

Meriwether stopped walking, "What's that supposed to mean?"

Daniel shrugged and kept walking, hands stuffed in his pockets. Meriwether couldn't stand it!

"Wait!" she yelled running to catch up. "What do you mean, Daniel? Sorry I was mean."

"I'm not stupid, you know," he said crossly, eyebrows furrowed.

Oh, great, thought Meriwether. *What have I done now?* "I know you're not stupid, Daniel. Please . . . I really am sorry . . . . Please tell me what you mean."

Daniel shrugged again, looking surly, "Saw 'im get up an' walk around is all . . . the night we found you . . . ."

"What?" Meriwether couldn't believe it. Was he that much worse off than he had been just a week ago? Is that what she'd done to him?

"Look, that's pretty," said Daniel, pointing to a

distant green field dotted with rolled up bails of hay.

Meriwether looked where he was pointing but barely saw it, "Yeah."

"I wouldn't mind a farm one day," Daniel said dreamily. "I like the fresh air and how the houses are spread far apart."

Meriwether was brought out of herself and thought guiltily of the dingy street in Oxford where Daniel lived with his mother. Suddenly the distance between them seemed even greater than ever. She looked at her watch, "Oh my gosh, we'd better hurry back if we're going to go with Jacob!"

"Do you really want to go?" asked Daniel, staring transfixed at the field.

"Yeah, I do!" Meriwether grabbed his arm and pulled him along. "I want to see where Dr. Willowsby lives!"

Chapter Sixteen

Hawkshead was a medieval sort of village of white washed houses and odd, winding streets; a sharp contrast with the dark trees and dramatic rises and fells surrounding the lakey hamlet. Meriwether and Daniel walked the high street and shopped the windows of bakeries, general stores, grocers, and haberdasheries while Mr. Greene delivered his eggs. People she had never met nodded at Meriwether. They, at least, seemed to know who *she* was.

Across the street, Meriwether could see Thorpe's and its display of fine woolens and tartan accessories. She wanted to bring Grandmother home a souvenir, and Holly too if she could find something good, so she left Daniel, intently watching an operating train set wind through its hills and tunnels in a toy shop window, and crossed alone to the clothiers.

An impeccably dressed, sallow faced man greeted her as she entered the shop and kept a careful watch on Meriwether as she ran her hand lightly over the stacks of soft blankets and sweaters pillared neatly on shining mahogany shelves. Although she saw many pretty things, Meriwether did not find anything that she thought Holly would like. It was almost never cold enough to wear wool in Texas . . . unless it was a purely outdoor activity. The schools and churches cranked up their heat in the winter, and where else was there for a twelve year old to go?

For Grandmother, however, Meriwether found a beautiful plaid throw in the muted russets and warm autumn colors that she loved. With a pang of homesickness, Meriwether imagined Grandmother cozying up with it in her chair in the den. She bought the throw, the sallow man seemed surprised, and returned to where Daniel still stood, gaping at the train set.

"Always wanted one of those," he breathed, making little fog marks on the glass.

"A farm and a train set," Meriwether said, smiling.

"Every young man's fantasy," grinned Daniel. "Oy, when'd you buy that?" he asked, indicating the bag she held in her hand.

"While you were drooling over the train," she laughed.

Daniel reached inside the bag and shifted over the tissue paper. "Very nice," he said, rubbing a fold of the throw between his fingers.

"It's for my grandmother . . . the one in Texas," Meriwether clarified. This was getting confusing. She was going to have to come up with something to call Mrs. Meriwether, but, as "Grandmother" was already taken, nothing else seemed quite right.

"There's Mr. Greene," pointed Daniel as the old man emerged from the market. They went over to meet him and help him load the empty crates into the back of the truck.

Greene closed up the tailgate and shook out his cap, "Mrs. Meriwether told me t' take you to lunch, . There's

Remmy's . . . but it's awful fancy . . . an' then there's The Royal George . . . more of a local sort o' place . . . ."

Meriwether looked down at her Texas Tech sweatshirt and jeans, "The Royal George sounds good to me." Jacob nodded and they climbed into the truck. Now was her opportunity. "Jacob, where do the Willowsbys live?"

Jacob kept his wrinkle lined face forward, but he cut his eyes warily toward Meriwether. "Up the way," he answered cryptically.

Meriwether wasn't going to let it go. "Can we drive by? I'd like to see it. Mary said they live in a great big house."

Jacob grunted, "An' what else did Mary say?"

Meriwether looked at him innocently. "Nothing. If it's that big a deal . . . ."

Jacob grunted again, but he started driving. Meriwether did not know if he would take them by the house or not, but she thought it best to leave well enough alone.

"This is the place," growled Jacob with a sideways jerk of his head as they drove slowly past a large, two story house made of white stucco with black shutters, half hidden by a wild and overgrown garden. It was probably beautiful in the summertime, but now the vines that webbed the house were leafless and brown, encasing the plaster in an eerie cocoon.

"Yikes," said Daniel.

But Meriwether didn't really care what the place looked like. Her purpose was to try and catch a glimpse of Mrs. Willowsby, Lillian Meriwether's mad sister. It was a long shot, Meriwether knew, but worth a try.

Her eyes swept the house. Even in the daytime, it looked dark, deserted. Heavy curtains covered most of the windows, and leaves lay where they fell on the front walk. Then, out of the corner of her eye, Meriwether saw a bit of movement from an upstairs window. Jacob was driving slowly by, but by the time she'd looked back to get a closer look, they were past the house. All she could see was the faint swish of the curtain as it fell back into place.

She shivered despite herself, "Double yikes."

The atmosphere of The Royal George was smoky and dense. At 12:30 it was packed to capacity and they were lucky to find a table: a great, thick topped slab of oak with decades of initials and expletives carved into its round face. Meriwether highly doubted this was what Mrs. Meriwether had had in mind when she suggested lunch.

That it was the local spot was obvious . . . and it was humming. Daniel eyed a group of girls in short skirts and too much eyeliner standing in a pack at the bar, smoking cigarettes and laughing loudly. Meriwether found herself wondering prudishly why the girls were not in school.

She coughed slightly and Daniel averted his gaze, looking somewhat sheepish. Nevertheless, she noticed him continue to sneak looks at the girls throughout the meal, when he thought no one was looking.

People kept gawking at them. Meriwether knew they must be putting two and two together, just like the people on the street, realizing who she must be because of Jacob and his connection with the Meriwethers.

The waitress set a steaming, golden potted pie, the crust hugging the sides of the dish in which it was baked, in front of Meriwether. She cut into it with her fork and the pastry crumbled flakily into the piping hot middle.

Meriwether blew on it for a while until it cooled enough to take a bite . . . yum!

Jacob kept his head down, enjoying his plate and his pint. When he'd finished, he pushed his empty plate away, took a pouch of tobacco from his pocket and rolled himself a quick cigarette. He blew his smoke away from Daniel and Meriwether as they ate, one skinny leg crossed over the other, and squinted at a television set in the far corner of the bar. The sound was completely obliterated by all the noise in the pub, but he watched the tiny horses run in silence, joining in the general *Hurrah!* as the lead horse crossed the finish line.

He mumbled something as he stood up and wove through the tables toward the bar. A fat man in a much wrinkled suit got up from his stool, and Jacob took his seat. Meriwether bent low over the table, "Did you see her?"

Daniel looked at the laughing girls and then back at Meriwether, a curious expression on his face.

"Not *her*," big eye roll, "Mrs. Willowsby . . . at the house . . . in the upstairs window."

"Oh," said Daniel . . . *was that a blush? . . .*, "yea . . . uh . . . no. You saw somebody?"

"I think so," Meriwether explained. "I saw some movement in the upstairs window -- just as we were passing. I don't really know that it was her . . . I'm just assuming because it's the middle of the day."

"Creepy," said Daniel.

"Yeah, I know. That's why I asked Jacob to drive us by. I wanted to see if I could get a look at her."

"I thought you must be up to something," grinned Daniel.

Meriwether shrugged, "Yeah, well, I didn't really . . . see her, that is."

Daniel shoved a huge bite into his mouth, "Why would you want to? She's crazy isn't she?"

"I know." Meriwether picked at a piece of burnt on crust that clung to the side of the dish. She didn't really understand the desire herself, but ever since she had learned that Dr. Willowsby's mother was her grandmother's sister, she'd been a bit fixated on the woman.

What had driven her mad?

Was mental imbalance something that ran in that side of the family? . . . that was something Meriwether felt she had a right to know.

Why did her husband keep her locked away in the house?

And why did young Dr. Willowsby continue to live at home? . . . . To help his father, or for some other reason entirely?

On the questions ran, and a glimpse of the Willowsby house had done nothing to quell them.

"I just get the feeling she's important is all," said Meriwether to her hands as she ran them lightly over the marred surface of the table.

"Important? How?" Daniel squinted at her quizzically. His warm brown eyes glinted gold in a beam of sunlight that had somehow managed to pierce the grimy front window of the pub. Meriwether was afraid to meet his gaze . . . afraid of what he might read in her eyes. She shrugged.

"I don't know. It's just weird, you know, now that I've met my grandparents . . . they just don't seem **that** bad. I can't get why they treated my mother the way they did. It doesn't make any sense. I obviously can't ask them about it. And I can't ask my mother. Dad's already told me his side of it . . . . I just wish I could talk to Mrs. Willowsby. Maybe she remembers something that could help me understand." Meriwether faltered and said in a suddenly small voice, "I've never talked to someone mad before."

"I could go with you," Daniel said bravely from his side of the table.

"Oh, Daniel, would you?" Meriwether's eyes shone brightly with emotion, although she absolutely refused to succumb to tears and embarrass herself.

"Do you want to go now, or wait for another day?"

Meriwether was startled. Speaking to Mrs. Willowsby was a hypothetical ...something she had imagined herself doing ...but never really thought she would. Daniel, however, was a very black and white sort of person. He didn't think about doing things . . . he did them. They both looked over to where Mr. Greene sat and noticed the bartender handing him a freshly filled, foamy pint. Greene's attention was deeply focused on the little screen behind the bar. Looking at one another, Meriwether and Daniel rose as one from their table and exited The Royal George.

Meriwether's heart beat fast in her chest and adrenaline pumped like an energy drink in her veins. What they had just done both scared and excited her. "We have to hurry," she said. Daniel set off a quick pace and Meriwether trotted along behind him. She was surprised when he climbed into Mr. Greene's truck. "What are you doing?"

"He always leaves the keys under the driver's seat," explained Daniel calmly.

"We can't steal his truck!" exclaimed Meriwether, half-way in and half-way out of the vehicle.

"We're not stealing it," said Daniel, still in that infuriatingly calm voice. "We're just borrowing it. You saw him . . . . He'll never know . . . as long as we hurry."

Meriwether felt sick to her stomach, but they'd already come so far. She had an opportunity, and she was going to take it. "Can you drive?" she asked, climbing into the seat and slamming the door.

Daniel grinned. His eyes twinkled. "Oy," he said.

Meriwether wasn't good with directions, and she couldn't have told you in a million years how to get back to the Willowsby house, but apparently Daniel had been paying attention. Moments later, they were pulling up to its spooky front. "What do we do, just ring the bell?" wondered Meriwether out loud. She was very nervous. It was broad daylight, but a gloom seemed to hang over this place. She shivered. Daniel pressed the bell with his thumb.

They could hear it through the door, echoing across the house. They waited for a full minute, but nobody came. Daniel shrugged and rang the bell again. Meriwether kept a close eye on her watch. They'd been gone less than ten minutes, but she knew that they needed to hurry. "Let's just try the door," she said in a low voice. "I don't think she'll answer."

Meriwether fully expected the door to be locked . . . was almost hoping for it because that would mean they could turn around and go back to the pub . . . so she was surprised when the knob turned easily in her hand. She looked at Daniel. He took a deep breath, and they entered the house.

The house seemed clean enough . . . Meriwether supposed they had a housekeeper . . . but it was messy. Newspapers strewn across the sofas and side tables, half empty cups of coffee sitting about making rings on the furniture, a jumble of overcoats, umbrellas, and hats in the entry. For all that, it was not unpleasant. It looked lived in at least -- not deserted like its exterior. But the movement she had seen had been in an upstairs window.

"Mrs. Willowsby?" Meriwether called as Daniel followed her up the stairs. *Hurry*, Meriwether kept telling herself, but her legs seemed to have a will of their own. She was deeply aware of the hour and was sure that one or both of the doctors Willowsby would arrive home any minute for a quick lunch.

There was no answer, but Meriwether could hear some odd clunking noises . . . a sound like a door closing . . . shuffling feet, "Intruders!" sang out a high, thin voice. At the top of the stairs appeared an old woman with streaming white hair. She was dressed in a pink house coat pulled tight against her tiny frame and strapped over a nightgown with a high, ruffled collar. Her thin arms held a baseball bat above her head, and in her eyes was a mad gleam. "State your name and business!" she cried, arms trembling.

Meriwether and Daniel froze where they stood. Meriwether's voice was shaking almost uncontrollably, "I . . . I'm Meriwether Knight . . . Felicia Meriwether's daughter. I . . . I wanted to ask . . . ." But that was all she was able to say. Mrs. Willowsby's eyes grew round like sockets, and her face turned an ever paler shade of white.

Her arms fell, the baseball bat clattered heavily to the floor, her body seemed to implode, crumpling to the ground in a dead faint.

Daniel felt for a pulse and found one, "She's okay. Let's get out of here!"

"But . . .," Meriwether hated to leave her like that.

"C'mon!" shouted Daniel desperately, pulling her down the stairs.

In no time at all they were sitting back at their table in The Royal George. Jacob had never noticed them gone, and it was almost as if nothing had happened . . . but it had.

Electric silence surrounded them as they rode back to the manor. Jacob, quiet by nature, didn't seem to notice anything off, and if he did . . . opted not to mention it. Meriwether twisted cold hands in her lap, her insides churning. She wondered if Mrs. Willowsby would come to before someone found her, and then she imagined either her husband or her son coming home to find the woman passed out at the top of the stairs. What would she say? Would they believe her?

She'd never meant to cause more harm, and she silently berated herself for not thinking the situation out more clearly. At the same time, Meriwether was struck by Mrs. Willowsby's reaction to her. The look on her face was one of shock . . . disbelief . . . almost as if she'd seen a ghost. Despite everything, it only made Meriwether want to talk to her more.

Jostling along in the truck, Meriwether made a decision. Something strange was going on, and if she could she would get to the bottom of it.

When they got back to the house, Daniel and Jacob

set to work sweeping out the chicken coops and Meriwether, who would have helped if she hadn't had something to do, headed for the house. The upstairs was deserted, just as she'd hoped it would be. Mary tended to tidy her room first thing in the morning, and as far as she knew, hers was the only upstairs room currently in use. Although she had a pretty strong feeling about it, she'd yet to determine unequivocally whether or not her room had been her mother's. If it had been, all the evidence had been removed . . . or had it?

Meriwether began a systematic search of every square inch of the room. There were some boxes at the top of the armoire, but they held only some old hats. Meriwether tried on a blue felt, 40's style woman's fedora, meant to be worn at a smoldering angle. She felt like a character from an old P.I. movie. All she needed was a slim, belted dress, some red lipstick, and a tearful tale to tell . . . truth or lies, it didn't matter.

Under the bed was completely clean, and the dresser drawers held only the clothes Mary had unpacked for her. Meriwether pulled a chair to the window and felt along the top of the window frame. It was dusty, but nothing was hidden there. She even used all her strength to lift up the heavy mattress and look underneath it. No luck.

Meriwether sighed. She had been so sure she would find something. Well, there were plenty of rooms to search. Maybe this room hadn't been her mother's after all. She carefully packed the hats away and stood on tip-toe to return them to their shelf at the top of the armoire. As she pushed back the box containing the blue fedora, it hit against something at the back of the closet. The hat box would not go back as far as the others had gone.

Curious, her heart racing slightly, Meriwether fetched the chair she had used to check the window frame and pulled it up to the open armoire. It was a long way back, and she could hardly reach, but a last she felt it . . . a book of some sort, with a soft leather cover. She slid it along the shelf with the tips of her fingers and wiped the book on her sweatshirt. It had been back there a long time.

On the cover, embossed in gold against the green, was the name **Felicia Meriwether**. At first, Meriwether thought it might be a Bible, but when she opened it up, she gasped. A dated entry . . . and the words, Dear Diary, ... Oh, it was too good to be true!

Knock, knock!

Meriwether shoved the diary back into the recesses of the armoire and clamored down from the chair. "Come in!" she sang, trying to act as if everything were normal.

"Tea in the kitchen," smiled Mary, peeking her head around the corner of the door.

Meriwether nodded, "Okay, just let me wash up."

Mary closed the door and Meriwether looked wistfully toward the diary. *Later*, she told herself. Her curiosity would have to wait.

Chapter Seventeen

Small and silent, Meriwether sat like a china doll in the middle of the huge four-poster bed that dominated the room. The evening was in early eclipse, and a chill breeze rustled the linden leaves outside and whistled through a small crack in the ancient leaded glass of her window. Like a glimmer of hope in a dark world, a single lamp lit the gloom, throwing ghostly shadows across the cold stone floor.

Meriwether pulled the covers up to her chin, curled on her side toward the lamp, and with icy fingers turned the precious pages that lay open before her.

She was closer now than she had ever been to knowing the woman who had sacrificed her health, and ultimately her life, to ensure Meriwether's own. She'd had so many questions . . . for so long. Her father had tried, but it was difficult for him to talk about her.

Besides, Meriwether mused, *how much could one person really know another anyway?* Only in the most unguarded of moments do we see in others anything but what we're meant to see.

The gentle in and out of her breath, the delicate rustling of the pages, the creak of branches in the wind, . . .

May 17.

Dear Diary,

I thought I heard a noise. At first I thought it was the wind, but then I listened harder and -- no, there it is again -- and it's definitely not the wind. Could it be Athena? I've often worried about her prowling around at night, but she absolutely refuses to stay in the house. She is very clever, and can find her way out of most any situation -- but if it's Athena she must be hurt because I've never heard her make quite that sort of noise before.

What was that? I think she's in trouble, and it's starting to rain! Better climb *down the tree and try to find her. Mother will murder me if she finds out.*

Not Athena. Athena was sitting on my bed when I climbed back into my room.

Oh diary, it was The Woman in White! I saw her in the trees, close to Jacob's wall. I saw her, and now I'm going to die....

. . . a low moan, a bone chilling wail . . . Meriwether sat up straight in bed and waited. Yes, there it was again. She swung her legs onto the floor and, keeping to the shadows, crept across the room to the columned safety of drapery folds.

    The thick glass made everything fuzzy, and even as Meriwether stared wide-eyed into the night she heard the sound again -- but couldn't see. Holding her breath, she reached behind the curtain and cranked the window open an inch.

    The park was bathed in struggling silver light, but the weak moon could not touch the inky blackness of the trees that marked the far border of the manor grounds.

    What was that?

Meriwether's heart was pounding, the metallic taste of adrenaline invaded her mouth, she saw something. Something white gliding through the trees.

For a long moment, Meriwether stood there -- frozen -- fear rooting her to the spot. Images and words flipped through her mind like clips from a movie.

. . . stay out of the trees
. . . holding hands, **go on***, a push and a scream*
. . . The Woman in White
. . . Artemis curled on the makeshift grave
. . . in danger, be careful
. . . and now I'm going to die.

Shaking, Meriwether pulled her sweatshirt back on and laced up her trainers. She'd never make it out the front door at this hour, and there was only one other way that she knew of; her mother had done it, and she'd seen Artemis do it a hundred times. She cranked the window out some more and reached for the limb that the cat leapt to so easily. Grabbing it, she gave the branch a good shake . . . seemed sturdy enough . . . and taking a deep breath, she left the safety of window sill, of lamp lit room, and went alone into the night.

The branches creaked perilously beneath her weight as she carefully made her way down the tree. Oh, how she wished she had time to go and find Daniel! In the distance she could see the glow of lights from the windows of the little cottage, but she knew that she had no time to waste. Whatever was out there might disappear if she didn't hurry.

Athena . . . Athena must have been her mother's cat . . . and she must have used the tree and the window to get into Felicia's room all those years ago. The thought made an odd chill creep up Meriwether's spine. Time and space seemed to have gotten all muddled up somehow. Who was she, anyway? Meriwether . . . or Felicia? Was this really happening . . . or had she fallen somehow into a dream, a memory locked inside the pages of her mother's diary? She shook her head and pinched her forearm. Looking down, she saw Artemis padding silently along at her side, "Meow," he said as their eyes met.

"Shhh," whispered Meriwether, grateful beyond measure for his company. He'd brought her back to herself, and she longed to grab him up and give him a squeeze, burying her face in his comforting, soft fur -- but she was afraid she would sneeze.

"Ohhh . . .," there it was again, that same low moan she'd heard from her window. They were nearly to the trees now, and as much as she hated to, Meriwether knew they would have to go in.

Whatever it was was getting louder; it sounded like weeping. Meriwether followed as best she could, using Artemis, moonlight reflecting off his white coat, as her flashlight. Meriwether had never been this way before. She'd always headed for the cliff that looked out over the water, but the sounds she followed led her away from the cliff and further into the trees.

The weeping was now distinct. Meriwether felt every nerve on end. It was cold out, but she barely noticed it, and then, through a line of trees she saw a clearing. In the clearing was a high stone wall, covered in vines, and in front of the wall was a stone bench, and on the bench was a woman, a woman all in white, crying as if her heart would surely break. Her face was in her hands, and as Meriwether stepped out toward her, her foot snapped a twig that lay in her path. The woman looked up, her face as white as her hair and her gown, and leaping from the bench, she disappeared into the wall.

Meriwether raced forward, "Wait!" But the woman was gone. Meriwether stood in the moonlight that fell like a ray on the little clearing. Artemis jumped lightly to the stone bench and began cleaning his ears. There was nothing else for it but to head back to the house.

Chapter Eighteen

Next morning, Meriwether reluctantly rolled out of bed with the sun. Her body ached after last night's travail, and she hadn't slept well. What she had witnessed haunted her. Had she seen a ghost, the same ghost her mother had seen all those years ago? She'd already decided to go back to the wall during daylight hours and get a closer look. In the moonlight, the woman appeared to have simply vanished, but she had seemed real enough before that.

But first things first, this was the morning she was to ride around with her grandfather and visit the estate. She dressed carefully in dark corduroy pants, walking boots, a bright pink button down shirt, and an oilskin barn jacket with deep front pockets. She pulled her hair back into a pony-tail and went downstairs in search of Col. Meriwether. Mrs. Cook met her at the bottom of the stairs and handed her a covered basket filled with warm breads and a thermos of tea. "Col. Meriwether's already out front. Hurry up now, doan't want t' keep 'im waitin'!"

Meriwether walked out the front door to find her grandfather climbing creakily into a vintage pick-up, meticulously maintained and in mint condition. It was shiny, and red, and the walls of the bed were made of waxed wooden slats fitted together like a fence. She noticed he was without the wheelchair and she remembered what Daniel had said. *He must just use it when he's feeling particularly weak or trying to save up his energy*, she thought.

He smiled when he saw her, "Good morning, Meriwether! Right on time . . . excellent. And I see Mrs. Cook's packed us some goodies . . . good, good . . . . Climb in, my dear . . . a beautiful day for it if I do say so!"

Meriwether returned his smile, "I love the truck! I've never seen one in real life before."

"Thank you," Col. Meriwether ran his hand lovingly across the dash. "Had the old girl for more years than I care to recall. I don't get much opportunity to take her out anymore, so this is a real treat for me . . . get to show off the two prettiest girls around . . . and don't you go telling Mrs. Meriwether I said that either," he said with a wink.

Meriwether laughed and crossed her heart.

"First I'll take you to one of the farms. I want you to meet the Neelys. They've been here with us for three generations and are excellent tenants. It's a symbiotic relationship, you understand . . . landlord to tenant . . . tenant to land . . . when one takes care of the other, we all benefit."

Meriwether nodded and listened as her grandfather talked and talked. He knew so much, and she felt as if she were trying to cram it all in her head the night before a big exam. How was she going to remember all this? It was important stuff too. People's livelihoods were at stake. She couldn't do it . . . couldn't handle it . . . couldn't . . . .

"Meriwether? You look a bit overwhelmed," said Col. Meriwether as they pulled up in front of a small white cottage.

Meriwether nodded, "I am, a bit. I'm afraid that I'll forget everything you're telling me. I don't want to mess it all up."

"Don't worry," he said reaching across the bench seat and laying a tremulous hand on her knee. "You'll have your trustees, and you'll have Lillian. You're a smart girl, I can tell. You'll do just fine. It's important to listen to the people around you, but in the end, you must simply do what you consider best. I believe in you, Meriwether, and I believe I've made the right decision in choosing you."

Meriwether gulped, "Thank you, sir. I'll try not to let you down."

"You won't," smiled Col. Meriwether. "Now let's go meet Jack and Helen Neely. I called and told them we were coming so we'd catch Jack at home."

By the time they got back to the manor, the long shadows of evening had fallen and Col. Meriwether was very, very tired. Meriwether had begun to worry about him earlier that afternoon. His face had turned an alarming shade of gray and his movements gradually became slower and slower. She'd tried to convince him to return home, saying that they could come back the next day and finish the tour . . . but he would hear nothing of it. He'd set out to show her the property and that was what he intended to do.

Meriwether helped her grandfather to the door, where he was met and fussed over by a solicitous Mrs. Meriwether and Mrs. Cook. As she helped him inside, Mrs. Meriwether threw a scathing look at Meriwether over her husband's shoulder. Clearly, she considered his depleted condition to be all her granddaughter's fault. Meriwether felt scandalized, but she was really too tired to get worked up about it. She shrugged it off and trudged up to her room where she found a sandwich under a large silver dome.

      She peeled off her clothes and ran the hot water as she devoured the sandwich, eating the last few bites as she sunk down into the steaming depths of her bath.

Chapter Nineteen

Meriwether woke up later than usual, little pools of sunlight swimming their way through the thick glass of her windows. Despite being tired, she'd stayed up late into the night reading her mother's diary. She thought it a bit odd that no one had woken her for breakfast, and her stomach was growling angrily after yesterday's light fare, Helen Neely's lamb chops being the only real meal she had enjoyed . . . a sandwich hardly counted as dinner in Meriwether's book. She pulled on a long sleeved tee and some sweat pants, and making sure the diary was well hidden, skipped downstairs for breakfast.

She saw Dr. Willowsby gliding morosely through the entry.

"Is Grandfather okay?" asked Meriwether, concerned. She had decided to call him "Grandfather".

Dr. Willowsby looked up at her with dark, serious eyes, enormous in his pale face, "Your grandfather is very ill, Miss Knight."

"Meriwether. Please, call me Meriwether."

"Yes . . . Meriwether," he hesitated, looking down the corridor, "Perhaps you'd best come with me."

Dr. Willowsby's black traveling coat rustled as he walked, and he brushed the hair from his eyes. His fingers were long and delicate, like a pianist's. Meriwether remembered seeing a piano at the Willowsby house, and she wondered if he played. Then she wondered with a jolt whether or not his mother had spoken of their encounter. The thought made her feel slightly queasy. What would he say to her? Was he terribly angry?

He led her to right outside her grandfather's room, which was bustling with quiet activity. Mrs. Meriwether was ordering people about in whispers, and when she saw Meriwether, delivered her a look of such malevolence that Meriwether actually winced.

"Thank you for coming, Julian," she said in a tight voice, thin from exhaustion.

"Of course, Aunt Lillian. I came as soon as I could. I'll go in and see him now." Mrs. Meriwether nodded, and Dr. Willowsby let himself into the sick room.

Meriwether didn't know what to do, so she sat in a chair in the hall and waited for Dr. Willowsby to come back out. Hours passed, and still Meriwether sat. Mrs. Cook brought her tea and some cheesy biscuits, and Meriwether guessed she ate them . . . but she didn't really remember. At one point, Mrs. Meriwether went into the room, and she didn't come out again. She had refused to make eye contact with Meriwether after that first telling glare, choosing to ignore her instead. *Fine by me*, thought Meriwether. She just wanted Col. Meriwether to be okay . . . and if he wasn't, then she felt like Mrs. Meriwether was right to hate her. He had overdone it yesterday . . . and he wouldn't have if she hadn't been there.

At ten to two, Dr. Willowsby and Mrs. Meriwether came out of the room. The young doctor had one arm around his aunt, as if supporting her. She looked haggard and shaken. Still, she did not look at Meriwether.

"Your grandfather wishes to speak to you, Meriwether," said Dr. Willowsby quietly.

Meriwether was ecstatic, "Then he's ... he's not...."

"He is alive, but just," murmured Dr. Willowsby. "Go . . . quickly."

Meriwether gulped as she stood and entered her grandfather's room. He lay in bed, propped up against several snow white pillows. He suddenly looked so old, so weak. Meriwether tried to swallow, but her throat had a great lump in it, and as he smiled and held out a trembling hand to her, she felt the tears rush down her cheeks. "Grandfather, I'm so sorry!" she cried as she went to him.

He took her hand and held it loosely in his own. "Sorry? Whatever for, my dear?" His voice came out in a hoarse whisper. He was very near to death.

"I . . . I'm sorry I made you tired yesterday. I'm sorry we didn't get to spend more time together. I'm sorry I didn't want to come in the first place," confessed Meriwether.

Col. Meriwether smiled, his walrus whiskers quivering, "My fault entirely . . . not yours.

"I want to give you something," he breathed, flinching with some inner pain.

Meriwether rubbed his veiny hand with her thumb, "But you've already given me so much."

"This is a secret," he said so lightly she could barely hear him. "Take this key," he took a key from the breast pocket of his dressing gown. "Go to the dresser and unlock the top right hand drawer." Meriwether did as she was told. "At the back of the drawer you will find a small object wrapped in a handkerchief." Meriwether fished around in the drawer, and discovering the article, held it up for Col. Meriwether to see.

He nodded, "Bring it to me."

She closed the drawer, locked it back, and walked back to her grandfather's bedside.

"Open it," he said.

Meriwether carefully unwrapped the handkerchief, until on her outstretched palm lay a small block of gold, shaped like a tombstone. Soldered to the top were the golden legs and curiously luminous green gold body of a large beetle. She picked it up. It was surprisingly heavy and emitted a strange heat that warmed her whole hand.

"A scarab amulet," wheezed her grandfather, "ancient Egyptian talisman . . . good luck . . . protection . . . yours . . . our secret . . . ." He reached out his hand and clasped it over Meriwether's, the amulet enclosed between their palms. He closed his eyes. Everything was very still, but Meriwether could see the slight rise and fall of his chest underneath the sheet; she knew he was just sleeping.

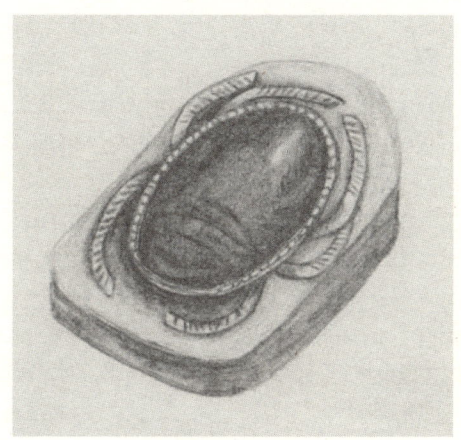

Wishing she'd worn something a little more bulky, Meriwether returned the jeweled box to its drawer and put the key in the breast pocket of Col. Meriwether's dressing gown. She took off her shoe and placed the amulet underneath the arch in her foot. It felt really weird, but at least it was undetectable. She kissed her grandfather on the forehead and left the room quietly. Mrs. Meriwether jumped up from the chair as Meriwether closed the door behind her.

"He's sleeping," said Meriwether.

Mrs. Meriwether nodded and went back into the room to keep watch. Meriwether walked down the hall, the amulet thunking awkwardly with each step, and out the front door. Col. Meriwether had said "our secret", but she thought he probably meant from Mrs. Meriwether, not from Daniel . . . and it was too strange not to tell somebody.

Once outside, Meriwether took the amulet from her shoe. It was, thankfully, none the worse for wear, and Meriwether turned it over and over in her hand as she walked, wondering how old it was and how her grandfather had come to own such a thing. Artemis appeared beside Meriwether as she walked.

"Where's Daniel?" she asked the cat, and followed the white tail into the orchard where Meriwether could smell the sweet scent of apple wood burning. Daniel and Mr. Greene were torching the mass of dead branches they had pruned days before. A long hose ran all the way from Mr. Greene's house just in case the fire got out of control, and the two of them were stationed on either side of the burn pile to keep an eye on things. This suited Meriwether just fine. It meant she could talk to Daniel in private without having to steal him away from his work.

"What's up?" asked Daniel as Meriwether and Artemis approached. "What've you got there?"

Meriwether held out her hand and let Daniel look at the amulet. "My grandfather gave it to me. Just now. Dr. Willowsby's at the house. They don't think he'll make it through the day."

"Whoa, I'm sorry Mer," said Daniel in a low voice. Meriwether looked up at him under wet lashes, a spark of something in her eye. "I'm sorry. I won't call you Mer if you don't like it."

"No, that's okay. I do like it. Holly calls me Mer . . . it was just strange for me to hear you say it," she tried to elucidate. "But I don't think I can call you Dan . . . or Danny . . . or anything but Daniel. I'm not good with nicknames."

Daniel smiled. "Can I hold it?"

Meriwether nodded, and closing her hand around the scarab, deposited it into Daniel's outstretched palm. She felt the loss of warmth immediately and shoved her hands underneath her arm pits.

"Cool," said Daniel appreciatively. "It's heavy."

"Yeah," nodded Meriwether. "And warm too." Daniel looked at her oddly, "Can't you feel it?"

Daniel closed his eyes, trying to focus. He weighed the object in his hand, then switched hands, then shrugged, "Nope, can't feel it." He handed the amulet back to Meriwether; radiating warmth instantly returning to her hungry hand.

"It's a scarab," Meriwether explained. "I've read about them, and it's something to do with the Egyptian sun god, Ra. Grandfather said it was for good luck . . . and protection. He also said it was a secret . . . like Mrs. Meriwether wouldn't like it if she found out. Weird, huh?"

"Yeah," agreed Daniel. "I bet he got it when he was stationed in Egypt."

"What?"

"Mr. Greene mentioned it one day . . . something about Col. Meriwether . . . during the war . . . in Egypt."

"What war?" Meriwether wanted to know.

Daniel shrugged, "I dunno. Wasn't really listening to tell you the truth."

Meriwether rolled her eyes, but she knew it wouldn't be too hard to find out. "I have to get back to the house," she said. Daniel nodded, his eyes focused on the fire. "C'mon, Artemis."

Chapter Twenty

Later that day, as Meriwether sat in the chair outside his room, Col. Meriwether died. She'd known it before Mrs. Meriwether came out to tell her because the amulet, hidden again in the arch of her foot, suddenly surged with heat -- the opposite of what Meriwether would have thought to happen. It was a comfort, and Meriwether felt certain that her grandfather was at peace. She did not fear this death.

As Meriwether drifted up to her room, she heard Mrs. Meriwether making the first of many necessary phone calls. Plans for the interment would keep her busy for several days, but Meriwether felt sure that all too soon the full force of her husband's death would hit the woman hard. Despite her shortcomings, Lillian had loved her Lionel very much.

Meriwether wished she could speak to her father, but instead she wrote him a letter telling him what had happened -- she wasn't sure Mrs. Meriwether would call -- and asking him to make arrangements for her return back to Texas. She'd done what she'd come to do. It was time to go home.

Mrs. Cook sent her up some supper, but she couldn't eat. Holding the talisman in her hand, she curled up on the bed and wrapped herself in a blanket, but she couldn't sleep. The weak light of a gray afternoon soon gave way to dusk's shadows, and as darkness fell around her she waited . . . and watched.

A cry pierced the night. She had known it would come, and though it struck fear into her very marrow, she forced herself to sit up from the bed and walk toward the window. The moon was full in the sky, and as Meriwether's pupils grew wide to let in its light, she saw what she was looking for.

She opened the window, and Artemis sat waiting for her on the branch, his tail swishing. He would be her guide. Climbing out and down without a sound, Meriwether followed the cat into the trees.

She'd worn her coat, and she turned the amulet over and over again in her pocket as she walked. Her nose and cheeks stung with the cold. She thought of Daniel, glad he was safe in the little cottage. This was something she had to do alone.

Artemis knew where to go, and he led them to the clearing they had visited just two nights hence. And, just like before, The Woman in White sat on her bench, weeping and wailing as if her heart would break.

Meriwether gulped, and clenching the amulet in her fist, letting its warmth permeate her hand and steal up her arm, stepped out from the trees and into the pale pool of moonlight.

As she did it, the woman looked up. Her face was ghostly white and as Meriwether took another step toward her, she stood and cocked her head to one side, like an animal determining friend or foe. "Felicia?" the woman whispered, stretching out her arms toward the child.

Meriwether took another step, "I'm Meriwether, Mrs. Willowsby. Felicia was my mother."

"My child, my own dear child," crooned Mrs. Willowsby, smiling through her tears. "You've come back to me."

She was suddenly lithe, like a young girl herself, and skipped toward Meriwether, taking her by the hands and swinging her about. She laughed and threw her arms about Meriwether, pulling her back to the bench, "You naughty thing! Where have you been all this time? Mummy's been worried."

Mummy? What was she talking about? wondered Meriwether.

"No one would tell me where you had gone," Mrs. Willowsby was pouting, her white hair standing about her face wildly. "Did Lillian send you away to school? She never did want me near you. Afraid you might find out, you know."

"I am in school, Mrs. Willowsby, but . . . but I'm Meriwether, not Felicia."

"And your father dead, poor thing. You must have come back for the funeral."

Meriwether was shaking. The woman was completely mad. "I . . . you mean Grandfather? Yes, I . . ."

Mrs. Willowsby began to rock back and forth. Her hands dropped Meriwether's and wrapped themselves about her own body for comfort, "And I . . . oh, but he never knew. . . we never told him . . . ."

Meriwether watched in horror as Mrs. Willowsby succumbed to her grief. She did not even seem aware that Meriwether was sitting there beside her.

"Wondered what had happened to his Lillian, didn't

he . . . there one minute . . . gone the next . . . a nasty trick, I'd say . . . and my baby, my sweet, sweet baby . . . .," Mrs. Willowsby wept, rocking and pulling at her hair. Meriwether stood up and backed away, backed into somebody.

Long fingers closed around her shoulders and held her in place as she tried to run.

"Let me go!" screamed Meriwether, struggling against the iron grasp.

The hands released her, and Meriwether ran for the safety of the trees, but she heard no footsteps follow. Once she was under their protection, she turned to see Julian Willowsby gently pulling a coat around his mother's shoulders, easing her distress with his low, gentle voice. Meriwether crept back out into the clearing.

Dr. Willowsby looked up. "Help me," he said.

Meriwether took one side and Julian took the other. Mrs. Willowsby shuffled obediently between them. Her grief was spent, had sucked the life right out of her, and she was like a zombie, mute and dumb to the world around her.

With his free hand, Julian swept away the vines that covered the masonry and twisted a latch in a door that had been completely concealed. "Is this what they call Jacob's wall?" asked Meriwether, something clicking in her mind.

"It's what your mother and I called it," answered Julian. "Greene didn't build it . . . it stood long before his time . . . but he used to shoo us away from here, guard it almost . . . said it was haunted . . . and it was."

"Haunted by . . . ?"

"By The Woman in White," said Dr. Willowsby, breathing hard under his mother's weight as they made their way down a winding footpath tread into the hillside.

"Is Mrs. Willowsby The Woman in White?" Meriwether felt strange asking such a question, but the moon was full, and it seemed as if they were in a dream. In dreams, you could ask anything you wanted.

Dr. Willowsby paused, "My mother, I believe, has long haunted this place. Soon you shall learn why . . . but there are legends of a white lady that go far back . . . way before mother's time. I do not know if they are true."

"My mother saw her . . . a woman in white . . . she thought she was cursed . . . that she would die."

Dr. Willowsby looked at her curiously, "How do you know this?"

Meriwether tried to concentrate on her footing so she would not fall. They were practically carrying Mrs. Willowsby by this point. "I found her diary . . . or one of them . . . in my room."

Julian scowled, "She must have hidden one."

"What do you mean?"

"Lillian has eliminated almost every trace of Felicia's existence . . . except for the memories she could not erase . . . and you . . . there was always you."

Willowsby's words rang in Meriwether's ears as they struggled toward a light that never seemed to get any closer, no matter how long they walked. She remembered her dream, that other dream, remembered falling, and she tried to make sense of the things Mrs. Willowsby had said, but it was all too strange. Meriwether felt suddenly hollow, and the ground was no longer steady beneath her feet. Like shifting sand, everything she knew, or thought she knew was giving way beneath her. And as for what was real? -- Meriwether could not say.

On and on they stumbled. Mrs. Willowsby had begun to come to a bit, and she mumbled to herself quietly, stealing curious, confused glances at Meriwether. Meriwether could tell from her eyes that the fog in her mind had not lifted, and she grieved for the lost woman whom she felt must still be in there somewhere.

At last they came to an iron garden gate and what Meriwether recognized as the reverse of the Willowsby house. Julian let them in the back door, which led into the kitchen. "I'll turn on the fire in the front room. Mother's chilled to the bone," he said. "And then I'll make us some tea. Are you all right to sit with her?"

Meriwether watched as Julian settled his mother on the couch and covered her with blankets, smoothed her hair from her face. "I'm fine," answered Meriwether.

Meriwether took Mrs. Willowsby's hand and patted it as they both absorbed the flames that sprung up from the gas fireplace. Mrs. Willowsby smiled at her like a child, and then stared absently into the fire.

When Julian came back, he seemed ready to talk . . . which was good because Meriwether needed some answers. "It runs in the family, you know -- dementia. Mother's mother (my grandmother and your great-grandmother) was committed when she and Lillian were just girls. My father knew it when he married her . . . even saw early signs of it . . . but love often drives away caution. Twins, identical twins . . . . I can show you a picture."

Meriwether wasn't sure who he was talking about, but when he brought her the pewter framed portraits, she knew at once. In the first one, two little girls with curling blonde hair sat side by side on a photographer's carpeted bench. They both reached for the camera, or something the person behind it held out to them, their chubby hands meeting in air, cherubic faces and small white teeth gleaming with glee.

In the next, two beautiful young women in cap and gown smiled serenely at the camera. One looked like a mirror image of the other. "Do you know which is which?" asked Meriwether, studying the picture.

"I have no idea," confessed Julian. "Both mother and Aunt Lillian left school with a teaching degree, and this was a time when it was not terribly common for women to go to college, but Lillian never worked. Well, I say that . . . but then I'm getting ahead of myself. She married Lionel the summer after graduation, and mother taught at the grammar school here in Hawkshead for years before marrying my father."

"They're lovely," said Meriwether, still staring at the picture of the young women. They remind me of a picture I keep of my mother. Meriwether's hand closed around the locket at her throat. Julian noticed.

"May I see?" he asked. Meriwether nodded and opened the clasp for Dr. Willowsby. He smiled a sad sort of smile when he saw the brilliant picture of Felicia, laughing for her father. "Is this in Oxford?" Meriwether nodded again. "Yes, she was beautiful . . . and so happy . . . but all of the trouble began with her."

Meriwether looked up at Julian, her hazel eyes meeting his deep brown ones. "What do you mean?"

Julian sighed deeply and began his story. "It was during the summer when school was out. Mother waitressed at a local pub to earn some extra money over the long holiday, and some RAF pilots came in on leave. One of them, apparently, swept her off her feet, promised her the moon. She's refused to ever mention a name, but from what she's said in her rantings, he was someone very important, perhaps even royal. Well, as I say, he swept her off her feet . . . and then he left, promising to return and marry her . . . but he never did because he was killed. She read it in *The Times*, so he **must** have been important.

"By then, she knew she was going to have a baby, and times then were not like times now. Her life would be ruined. She would lose her job. She would have no way to care for the child. And then there was her sister . . . married, but unable to have a baby. They'd tried for years, and nothing had worked. The sisters agreed, and they switched places."

Meriwether felt her heart, which had been up in the vicinity of her throat, drop all the way down to the base of her stomach. She felt instinctively for the talisman in her pocket, turning it over and over in her hand, concentrating on its warmth to ground her.

"They never told anyone what they had done, not even Lionel. They simply switched and began leading one another's lives. Mother moved into Meriwether Manor, and Lillian came to mother's little cottage and taught school. Two or three months after your mother was born they switched back -- and if anyone suspected, as I believe my father, who delivered the baby, did -- no allegations were ever made. Scandal was completely averted . . . just as planned . . . but it ruined mother. She was never the same again . . . even when she married my father . . . even when she had me."

Meriwether could tell it cost Dr. Willowsby to admit

it. She wanted to say something to make him feel better, but she didn't know what.

"Oh, at times she was carefree . . . and clear . . . and wonderful!" continued Julian. "No one was more fun than mother when she was on – but, well you've seen her. She's confused, mixes up the past and present, wanders up to the manor and grieves the loss of her child . . . and of the man she came to love during the months she spent in his house."

"Is that why Mrs. Meriwether is the way she is?" asked Meriwether. "Because her sister fell in love with her husband?"

Julian shook his head slowly, "No. Lillian is the way she is because her husband fell in love with her sister."

Meriwether was confused, "But he never knew . . . ."

"But she did," explained Julian, "She knew, and it poisoned her."

"Your poor father," breathed Meriwether.

Julian nodded, "He never had a chance. But, like I said, I think he suspected the truth from the beginning. He knew she did not love him as he loved her. I believe he thought she would learn to love him . . . and she did . . . but not like she had the others. He could never, no matter how hard he tried, live up to those ghosts. And he could not slay her demons. She lives with them still, and they torment her."

Meriwether looked at Mrs. Willowsby who had fallen asleep beneath the blankets, her head resting on the arm of the couch. Her face looked calm and much younger; Meriwether could see in that face the woman from the photograph, could imagine her as she once was, and her heart ached with the tragedy of it all.

"She's my grandmother," said Meriwether haltingly. "You're my -- uncle. My mother's brother. Did you know, always?"

"No. Not until Felicia was already gone. Mother spiraled with her death, as you can well imagine."

"I . . . I don't even know her name," Meriwether reached out and smoothed away a lock of her grandmother's flyaway white hair.

"Lydia," murmured Julian. "Her name is Lydia."

Chapter Twenty-One

Meriwether helped Julian settle his mother out on the couch and accepted his offer to walk her back up to the manor. The moon was full -- they did not need a flashlight – and the climb was steep. For this, Meriwether was somewhat glad because it got her blood pumping, which helped her to stay warm beneath her woolen coat.

Julian had wrapped his neck with a scarf, a blaze of red against a background of black, and his breath was visible on the air. His pale skin shone in the moonlight and the night wind ruffled his black hair. He looked like a . . . .   Meriwether shivered despite herself. Vampires weren't real . . . or at least she sincerely hoped they weren't.

"What are you thinking?" he asked, breaking a long silence.

Meriwether answered without meaning to, "That you look like a vampire." She flushed mightily, glad of the night's cloak, as a small smile pulled at the corners of his mouth.

"There's no such thing, Meriwether," he said silkily.

Daniel sat up straight in bed. He'd been fast asleep,

but something had woken him up; a dream maybe? His t-shirt was soaked with sweat and he shivered as the cold air of his room made contact with the wet clothing. His heart was racing too.

This was something to do with Meriwether.

He shucked the tee and dressed as quickly and as warmly as he could. Careful not to wake Jacob, Daniel crept to the kitchen and silently slid open the drawer that held the knives. He opted for a small, sharp paring knife, afraid he might impale himself on one of the longer ones, and stuck it through his belt as he had seen Jacob do before.

He felt a bit silly, but he was not walking into that forest unprotected. No telling what kind of a mess Meriwether had gotten herself into now.

Meriwether swallowed hard. Something was off. "I know that!" she laughed -- nervous. Her voice trilled unnaturally, and like a bird, settled on a branch above their heads. Seconds later, she could still hear its eerie, hovering echo.

She grabbed for the amulet in her pocket. It was pulsing with heat. **Protection. In danger. Don't go in the trees. Oh, I hope you really work**, wished Meriwether desperately.

Artemis met Daniel on the front step. He looked up at the boy and swished his long white tail.

"Take me to her, Artemis," Daniel murmured.

The cat led Daniel along a path he had never traveled before. The way was clear because of the full moon, but Daniel felt strange. He took the knife from his belt and held it in his hand.

Meriwether, where are you?

Chapter Twenty-Two

On and on Julian and Meriwether walked, and Meriwether wondered how they had done it with Mrs. Meriwether between them. She tried to focus on the scarab and its warmth, and tried to fight back the terror that was rising inside of her. *Vampires aren't real. Vampires aren't real.*

Suddenly, a thought popped into her head; she felt compelled to ask it. "What happened to Athena?"

Julian stopped walking. He turned toward Meriwether with a curious expression on his face. "What do you know of Athena?"

"I . . . read about her in my mother's diary," Meriwether stammered, "and then w . . . uh, I found her gravestone on the cliff overlooking the lake."

Julian smiled, "Felicia loved that cat. White all over . . . beautiful."

"What happened to her?" asked Meriwether again, afraid he'd forgotten the original question.

"I drowned her," answered Julian in a soft voice that sent chills running down Meriwether's spine.

Meriwether backed away from her uncle, but he grabbed her arm and held her fast. His dark brown eyes looked black, and his handsome face was a mask of terrifying calm.

"Did . . . did she know?" trembled Meriwether in horror.

"Of course not," he smiled. "I put her in a tow sack, drowned her in the lake, let the body dry out, and then hid her beneath the rose bushes. Felicia never had a clue what had happened to her beloved Athena."

"You . . . you let her carve your initials on the marker . . . like you cared . . . ."

"Of course I did," he explained in his mad, calm voice. "She was my best friend."

Meriwether shrieked, "If she was your best friend — Why did you kill her cat?"

"It is a difficult thing to say why a child does anything, Meriwether. I would think that you might understand that, being not far from childhood yourself," his grip tightened imperceptibly on her arm. "I believe that I was feeling a bit left out, if you know what I mean."

Meriwether was scared, but she was also angry. "I most certainly do not know what you mean!"

He smiled indulgently. Meriwether checked for fangs. "Let me see if I can explain. Even as a child, or perhaps I should say, *especially* as a child, I could tell that I was not my mother's favorite. Of course I didn't understand *why* . . . I simply thought I wasn't good enough . . . that she doted on Felicia because she was her idea of the perfect child . . . or maybe because she had wanted a girl instead of a boy. Felicia was my playmate and my confidant. I loved her . . . and I also hated her."

Meriwether listened with eyes wide. Despite herself, she could imagine the pain of the boy Julian. It made her sick, but she actually felt sorry for him.

"I killed the cat because Felicia loved her. I wanted to cause her some pain . . . to compensate for my own."

Meriwether could feel an acidic tingle at the back of her throat. She kept her teeth clamped shut to keep from vomiting.

Julian assessed her slowly with his black eyes, "You make this all too easy, you know. I warned you to stay out of the trees."

Meriwether was instantly on high alert. Something had changed. He was talking about something else. "Wha . . . what do you mean?"

"I know why you came, and I know what Col. Meriwether said to you." Meriwether closed her hand even more tightly around the talisman in her pocket, but she realized that was not what he was talking about. "There are no Meriwethers left. You see, even you are not a Meriwether – not by blood. And who do you think is second in line to inherit the manor and its estate?"

Meriwether's wide eyes flattened into slits, "You are."

"Good girl! Very astute," he said, pulling her from the worn path and into the dense foliage of the trees. "As I said, you make it far too easy."

Meriwether was panting now, the faces of the people she might never see again racing through her mind. *What would he do with her out here . . . would he drown her in the lake too? He was a doctor. He would know how to conceal his crime. No one would ever know what had truly happened to her.*

Her father . . . her poor, poor father, and at the thought of him her heart sank. *He would never ever forgive himself for making her come. And Grandmother . . . what would Grandmother do without her?*

"Oy, there!" rang out a voice from somewhere a little further up the hill. "What's going on then?"

"Daniel?" Meriwether half choked, half cried. Julian was temporarily startled and dropped Meriwether's arm. She took her opportunity and ran for it. She screamed at Daniel, "Run!"

Daniel didn't need to hear it twice. He could see the wild fear in Meriwether's eyes and even though he didn't know what was going on, he could tell it was bad.

It took Julian but a second to recover, and he was after them. Artemis darted out in front, leading a winding way through the trees, deeper and deeper into the heart of the wood. There was a powerful stitch in Meriwether's side, but she dared not stop. She couldn't tell how far behind them he was, but she sensed that he was close — much, much too close.

Even in the moonlight, Meriwether thought she could tell where they were headed. She wondered at the wisdom of it even as her falling feet brought her closer and closer to the spot. She realized they were putting all their faith in Artemis. *I hope you know what you're doing, cat.* And then there they were, on the cliff overlooking the tarn, cornered between the ledge and a madman bent on murder.

"Dr. Willowsby . . . Uncle Julian . . . you don't want to do this," stammered Meriwether as he slowed to a stalk. "I don't even want it . . . I'll sign it all over to you . . . just let us go."

"Touching," smiled the good doctor. "I almost believe you might . . . but it won't work. All that legal mumbo jumbo, you know. Your trustees would never agree to it. Unfortunately, a death . . . or two," he said, looking at Daniel, "is required."

He walked slowly toward them. He was going to push them over the edge. Daniel bent low, paring knife in hand, ready to fight. "Run for it," he hissed through clenched teeth.

Meriwether jerked her head no, her eyes never leaving Dr. Willowsby, who was so close now she could reach out and touch him.

"Yes," he snarled.

"No!" cried Meriwether, turning her head toward Daniel. She gasped and stared beyond him into the trees at the edge of the clearing. Despite themselves, Daniel and Dr. Willowsby turned to see what had suddenly drained the blood completely from Meriwether's face.

A woman, glowing a translucent white, stepped out from the trees. The wind was up, but her hair and gown did not move, and her feet stepped not on the ground but on air. She raised a white hand and pointed it at Julian's heart, and her eyes held his as she glided toward them.

Meriwether pulled Daniel aside as Julian backed away from the lady. His face was ashen and his mouth made funny gaping noises like a suffocating fish. Closer and closer to the cliff's edge he inched, and still the phantom advanced, her piercing gaze a death sentence. He tottered. One more step and he would be finished.

The lady lowered her hand, and shifting her gaze, smiled at Meriwether and Daniel. Dr. Willowsby was released from her spell. Looking about wildly, he took one step forward, and in that instant Artemis was between his legs. He cried out in surprise as he stumbled and lost his balance. It was like slow motion, and his eyes met Meriwether's as he lurched back into unsubstantial air, his black coat billowing out from him as he fell, nothing but jagged rock to cushion his descent.

Meriwether and Daniel watched him fall, their eyes met, and they turned as one to the spot where The Woman in White had been just seconds before. She had completely disappeared.

Artemis wound his way through their ankles purring, and Daniel reached down to give his ears a rub.

"Good boy, eh," he said in a soft voice that nevertheless seemed much too loud. Artemis responded with a resounding, revving motorcycle purr, and they followed his swishing tail as it led them safely home through the trees.

Chapter Twenty-Three

"You okay?" Daniel nudged Meriwether with his elbow as she rested her temple against the cold glass of the train window, staring blindly into a sea of pea soup fog. The wild hills and fells, black lakes, and little whitewashed towns lay just beyond her reach; out of sight, perhaps, but never now far from her mind.

She shrugged without looking at him, "Okay, I guess."

The rhythm of the train had a hypnotic effect. Long gaps passed between their dialogue, but in context it seemed completely normal. Meriwether was thinking, thinking and trying to let it all sink in. Two funerals in two days, a round table meeting with her trustees (a somber lot to a man), and Mrs. Meriwether's guarded stares as she tried to assess what all Meriwether knew ...

Numb. Except for the warmth of the scarab as she turned it over and over in her hand, she felt absolutely numb -- completely overwhelmed.

Daniel, of course, knew her secret now. He hadn't said a word about it, though, and Meriwether wondered what he must be thinking. As if he'd read her mind he said, "I'm glad it's yours, you know. You'll do right by the place . . . when you're old enough."

His words were like a warming draught to her cold, foggy brain. Meriwether could feel herself coming back to life, "Thanks, Daniel," Meriwether said with a small smile. "It's all a little much."

"Aye . . . must be." The tone in Daniel's voice made Meriwether look up at him.

"Are **you** okay?" she asked, anxious for his thoughts. She didn't want the wedge to drive them apart so soon.

Conversation was picking up now. They were getting back on track. "Me? Oh, sure," he hedged with false bravado. "I was just thinking that someday I could come be your gardener. Old Greene isn't getting any younger, you know."

Meriwether fixed him steadily with large, dark eyes. Enough was enough. "I don't want you to be my *gardener*, Daniel. I don't want you to be my *anything* . . . except my friend. I know you're not going to listen to me. You're going to do exactly what you want to do. But I need to know why you quit school . . . and you haven't told me everything yet, I know it ... So out with it!"

Meriwether was steeled for Daniel's anger. She didn't care, as long as she got the truth. So she was surprised when he hung his head and replied, defeated, "Mum's getting married."

"She's getting . . . . Well, that's won . . . . Well that means . . . . Oh." It didn't take long to put it all together. She was marrying the oily little man Meriwether had met at her going away party last summer. *Ooh*.

"Yeah," Daniel's voice was dead. "Can't stand it really. The thought of living in the same house with him makes my skin crawl. I ... I thought that if I quit school ...

got away …I would feel better. But I don't, you know. I think, actually, I've made a big mistake."

"It's okay, Daniel," Meriwether felt sorry for him, but at the same time, eager to show her support. This was music to her ears. "It's not too late. You've hardly done anything at all. I bet you could re-enroll no problem!"

Daniel's brown eyes were pained as he looked up into Meriwether's. "You aren't listening. I can't live there with them. I've thought about it a lot, and I just can't."

Meriwether would not give up so easily. "Then stay with Mrs. Doone and my dad. I'm sure they would let you."

"Yeah, I'd thought of that . . . but what would I tell me mum? That would really hurt her feelings."

"Hurt her feelings more than you dropping out of school? I don't think so, Daniel."

Daniel shrugged, "Yeah, I guess."

"And you could say that your gran needs your help, which is true, and that you're interested in archaeology and that my dad had agreed to . . . to mentor you or something!"

Daniel bit his bottom lip as he thought, "Like an apprentice?"

"Exactly!" smiled Meriwether. "I mean, I don't know whether you're really interested in archaeology or not . . . but you could say it . . . to make your mom feel better."

"I am though – interested."

"Then it's settled. I'll talk to Dad as soon as we get back to Oxford. He'll know what to do. Don't worry Daniel. Everything is going to work out. You're going to be fine."

Daniel smiled and looked straight into Meriwether's blazing eyes, "Hey, that's supposed to be my line."